The Way of the Vihangwanah And The Rainy Season

A.V. Joshi

RIGI PUBLICATION

The Way of the Vihangwanah And The Rainy Season

A.V. Joshi

Originally published in the India

ISBN: 978-93-84314-01-9

Published by RIGI PUBLICATION
777, Street no.9, Krishna Nagar
Khanna-141401 (Punjab), India
Website: www.rigipublication.com
Email: info@rigipublication.com
Phone: +91-9357710014, +91-9465468291

Front Cover page Image designed by
Surendra Dadarao Deshmukh

Dedication

Dedication for this book is divided into three steps.

First to,
My family's mature support for my childish writing, including my Brother-in-Law and sister.

Second to,
My intimate friend A.R.Kene with whom, I have trodden all grassy paths of my native village and prof. Mr. Chinchole.

And,
Third to,
This eminent Nature who, gave me unpremeditated ideas of writing and inspired me to write with her charming quill.

- A. V. Joshi

"Full many a gem of purest ray serene

The dark unfathom'd caves of ocean bear;

Full many a flower is born to blush unseen,

And wastes its sweetness on the desert air."

by - Thomas Gray

The Characters in the Novel

1.	Mahina and Mooni	-	Mynah birds (wife and Husband)
2.	Raghu	-	The various coloured Parrot
3.	Lark	-	The Lark bird
4.	Bagga	-	The white male Heron
5.	Sona	-	The Owl bird
6.	Robin	-	The Robin bird
7.	Sugi	-	The female weaver bird
8.	Kite	-	The kite bird
9.	Kaka	-	The wild black Raven
10.	Koel	-	The Cuckoo bird
11.	Parinda	-	The pigeon
12.	Dove	-	The Dove
13.	Chidiya	-	The Sparrow
14.	Woodpeck	-	The woodpecker bird
15.	Gilhary	-	The squirrel
16.	Safeda	-	The white wild rat
17.	Eaglet	-	The Offspring of the eagle

★ As per Indian mythology the moon is treated as God (Masculine) Therefore in this perticular novel in the story of *The Legend of The Birds* The Moon is treated as God.

FIRST

That morning of *The Vihangwanah* could have been the usual one. But, that peace which was the identity of the vihangwahah, today had been hidden somewhere. There was yet some time to introduce the first appearence of The Sun to the Vihangwanah.

Gilhary (*the squirrel*) was running through the intricated branches of the *Palsah tree.* Her tail was as straight as a any brush and helping her to climb on the tall Palsah tree. Gilhary stopped on the one big bough, in front of a hole, which seemed to be closed with wooden-swoop.

"Mahina ! Mahina !" Gilhary called loudly, "Come out fast."

Soon the wooden swoop was opned from inside and Mahina *(Female mynah bird)* came out from her residence hole.

"What happend Gilhary! what is your intention to come here so early in the dawn time?" asked by Mahina.

"Something is very important to tell you." Gilhary said with haste, "No. There is no time to tell you what happened. It will be better that you come with me. Everybird of the Vihangwanah is coming under *The big Old Banyan tree.* You and Mooni (the husband of Mahina) come soon there, as you possible. I have to go now, Becasue, I have an important task." After saying this, she turned back and once again began to cross the uncontrollable branches of the Palsah tree.

Other hand *Robin* bird was flying to another side of the Vihangwanah. After some time, he landed on the thornfull branches of *A Babol tree*, with the help of his adept wings. The branch where he landed was the top branch of the tree. It was an impossible for unskilled bird to land on those branches of the Babol tree. The thorny branches of the Babool tree do not give any chance to commit a mistake. There also a hole in front of Robin as same as the tree hole which was present on the Palsah tree. This hole had also been closed by the swoop of wooden. Robin knocked the swoop with his black beak.

He has not to wait for a minute. The wooden swoop was opened and a Lark bird came out from inside.

"Robin, my friend, you are here, what a great surprise." Lark said, with surprise, "come with me inside, and have a breakfast".

But, Robin was not seemed to intersted in breakfast, he said, "No. No. Lark. This is not a time for breakfast you have to come under the big Banyan tree, by a side of the river. Assembly has been called out there. All birds are coming there. You do come there fast as you can. I have still some messages to convey. I have to go on with my duty. Please, come soon. Bye, Bye. This task is being completed by Gilhary and me."

"Okay! Okay! go ahead. I take littel breakf__"

"This is not time to have the breakfast," Robin did not listen even a word of Lark. He further said, "The matter is very serious indeed. You have to make haste.For God's sake." he spread his wings after that and leaped into air from the thorny branches of the Babool tree.

Before rising The Sun, many birds (i.e. Assembly members) were gathared under the big Banyan tree which was standing on the shore of the river. (There was only one river in the Vihangwanah.) Among those birds, there was a white Dormouse, whose eyes was black and brown (and was having a long white tale). They all were waiting for birds, which were yet to come. Soon, there came the fleeting sound of wings, and every present eye moved towards the red and brown sky. Chidiya (*The sparraow*) and Kite - *(The Kite bird)* were coming down collaborately.

"You both are getting late." Robin said, to chidia and Kite, when they touched their feet on grassy land at the meeing spot, under the shadow of the big Banyan tree.

"We both are really sorry." Chidiya said submissively, "I can't fly fast like Kite can. For me he did not fly with his normal speed. He had to wait for me and therefore we have got late."

"Okay no problem then." Mahina said "so, Robin why did you make us gathared here?"

"Because, we all have been invited on this place by Bagga." Robin told, with a little jump.

"Brohter Bagga, which type of meeting is this and so early in the morning. There was not notice before this meeting, was it? Or here is only I am who did not get any notice about this perticular meeting?" Woodpeck *(The Woodpecker bird)* asked, he was looking stress.

"Woodpeck not only you but, also I have not heard or got any notice concerned about this meeting ," Sona - (*The Brown coloured owl)* said, making his yellow eyes bigger, "My tree hole is very close to Bagga's Fig tree and even then he has told me nothing. Very soon my sleeping thim will be on. Because, The Sun has already been rising-"

"Please, be quite friends." Bagga *(The middle age male Heron)* requested with serious voice. Bagga was the biggest and tallest bird in the Assembly. "I have gathered you all here because; I have something to show you."

All birds and Two little animals *(Safeda and Gilhary)* were gazing at Bagga. Bagga looked them with stern look and walked towards *"The Abhata tree"* with his long legs. He stopped near the trunk of the tree and shown his either wing towards the bottom of the tree. Every body who were presented at that meeting, saw in that direction and they just kept staring there for some time.

There was laid a small white woollen swag, near the trunk of the Abhata tree. Anybody could have thought like this who would see that swag at the first time. But then, the Assembly members throught that, the white swag was breathing like any other living thing. That swag was not a swag of cotton or woollen indeed but, an offspring of a bird. But, at this time, it was in asleep.

"What is this?" Safeda -(the Dormouse) asked. He came two footsteps ahead.

"This is an offspring." Kaka (*The Black Raven*) answered.

"Auff! Kaka every one can see that, it is an offspring." Parinala *(The white pigeon)* said with nurvous tone, "But, question is where it came from?"

"Why are you asking me about it?" Kaka irritately said, "Ask to Bagga. He has gethered all of us here."

Now everybodey was looking at the Bagga, like he was an any queer thing.

"I had gone to river some time ago at time of dawn. You know that I accomodate or live on the Fig tree, which is standing by the next shore of the river. The Fig tree is very dear to me. At first hand I had gone to the west side of the river in the search of some fish. But, I have not got even one, that reason, I came on this shore of the river. I was looking for fresh fishes but suddenly I found this offspring sleeping laid under the Abhata tree. I could not think what I do? Eventually, I saw Robin here and after that I asked him to convey the messages to all of you."

Hearing this, Robin spoke, "I met Gilhary on a Jamoon tree and she happily took the half responsibility of my task. That reason I could easily complete my work. I heartily thank to Gilhary, for her quick support."

Gilhary was standing on her hind legs and looking at Robin very meekly.

"But, Gilhary why you did not come to me instead of Robin? your tree -hole is near to my tree- hole. You could have come early for deliver the message." Lark asked to Gilhary.

"Your opinion is right Lark, but your accomodation to having on the Babool tree and the Babool tree have thorns that reason, I can not climb on that tree with skill and therefore, I did leave this responsibility on Robin." Gilhary innocently pointed out her clarification Lark nodded his head positively.

Silent spread there for some time then Sugi - *(The female weaver bird)* asked, "But, which bird having this type of offspring?"

Again every eye fixed on the offspring, of white colour. Who had laid asleep with tucked his head in his white wings.

"Among us which bird possesses the offspring like this?" Parinda asked to everybody.

"Among us, only the -Heron species having this type of offspring. But, I think it is not belonged to my species." Bagga made a remark observelly, "It does not look like the Heron indeed." He went closer to the offspring.

"But, the Vihangwanah is being inhabited by only birds. It is the forest of birds so, the offspring can belong to any bird of the forest." Koel (*The cuckoo bird*) said in her melodious voice.

"Yes, Yes. It is right that this forest namely the Vihangwanah is inhabited by birds only." Lark came ahead and began to observe the offspring with his blue eyes. "- but, I think this offspring belongs to the bird which is not a part of the Vihangwanah as well as, he can not be found at surrounding region also."

The Lark had the great knowledge about everything. He was the adviser of the Assembly of the Vihangwanah also he was the president of the Assembly of the birds and sometime he used to make the right judgement of uncertain decisions. Everybody gave him respect. This time he was elected *first* time for the presidentship.

"Whose offspring is this?" Kite asked a question.

"This is not an offspring indeed. This is an eaglet and not of a common one eaglet. It belongs to the one of the rare species of the eagle family." Lark provided necessary information "But, how did he come here, in the Vihangwanah all alone?" Dove *(The Dove bird)* questioned.

"No one can make answer on it. When this eaglet got wake up then he will tell us a story of his travel to the Vihangwanah." Mooni, Mahina's husband went closer to Eaglet and said, "He will definitely tell us very important information about him."

They did not have to wait for long time for their answers, very soon Eaglet woke up and he astonished to see that so many birds were surrounded to him and observing him with curiosity. He stood on his small legs and fearfuly looking at the every bird, which were strangers for him. On his opinion they all were looking strange and different suddenly, his eyes stopped on Bagga and he reached to Bagga within in two jumps.

"Mother! Mother! Where are we?" He screamed on Bagga.

"What? I am not your mother, I am -" Bagga was saying something but without listening any answer from Bagga, Eaglet asked further, "-OH! Then are you my father?"

"No.No. I am not your father or Mother either." Bagga spoke hesitatingly "I am Bagga, a Heron."

After hearing this account Eaglet was looking amazed. He raised his head towards Bagga and told, "My father looks like you, same to same."

At the moment Parinda came two footsteps ahead, "Is your father as tall as Bagga?"

"No. definitely not. His legs are same like my legs and they even not so tall. But where he is and where I am?" question put down by Eaglet.

"You are at the Vihangwanah but, how did you come here." Sugi asked, springing her tail.

"I do not know that, I had left with my father for this long long journey the day before yesterday at night. I can not fly or you can say that I am not able to flap my wings with my own efforts. That reason, he had caught me in his claws. We stayed at this place yesterday (last) night. I was in the deep sleep and therefore, I could not see what happened then." Eaglet was telling the story of his travel then he asked, "But, where is my father?"

"Even you don't know where he is?" Lark asked in serious tone.

Eaglet nodeed his head negative and he was looking very disturbed.

"Where had you both been going to the journey?" Bagga questioned and waited for an answer from Eaglet.

"I don't have any idea about that. But, we were going to the Eastward." Everybody (Every bird and two animals) were seemed to be in great trouble. This was very harsh time for them. They could not understand the meaing of all this commotion.

"Okay. That is all right." Safeda spoke in has thin voice, "Where did you come from?"

"Our families live in deserts on highland. There is no forest or tree like these are or there is no birds like you are. Only we, mean the Eagles and our foes the Vultures dominate that deserts and the region.(That area is inhabitated by the Eagles and the Vultures only)," the eaglet told the information, "But, where am I at the moment? What is the name of this palce? I forgot what had you told sometime ago?"

"The name of this forest is *Vihangwanah* and this is the typically bird forest. The Vihangwanah is dominated by only birds and I think they are all here except one. There is no other species is the part of the Vihangwanah." Sona spoke after long interval of time. Abruptly having seen so strange bird; Eaglet frightened and he stepped away from Sona and reached more close to Bagga.

"AH .... I am sorry but, who are you, and why your eyes are so big and yellow and how can you move your eyes so speedly?" After reclined on the legs of Bagga, Eaglet asked to Sona, "- and how could you turn your head here and there so quickly?"

"Let me tell. He is Sona and he is an owl." Gilhary was telling to Eaglet, she was standing in hind legs. She had suddenly come out front and Eaglet looked her at first time. At that very moment Eaglet screamed loudely and made his way between the long legs of Bagga, "What is it? So peculiar?" Hearing this remark from Eaglet everybody laughed even Gilhary herself also.

"Do not fear me son. I am not going to harm you any way. I am a squirrel and everyone call me Gilhary, with love."

Having heard this information Eaglet relieved for instance and came forward to observe Gilhary from legs of Bagga. He was observing Gilhary with his small black-Brown eyes, having taken advantage from this situation; Mahina spoke to Lark, "I think, he did not see any other bird except his father. He is looking us (these types of birds) for the first time."

Lark noodded his head affirmative and said in agreealbe voice, "He is very small indeed and only way that we can get history of his life by asking him about his father. He can give us some important information."

Some surrounding birds flapped their wing for consentment. *(Flapping of wings was the symbol of applause and agreement too)*

Mahina came closer to Eaglet and asked, "Do you have any brother or sister?"

Eaglet not made any answer but, only noodded his head negative. He was still by the side of Bagga .Eaglet was thinking that Bagga might be the any bird of his eagle family.

"Where is you mother?" Sugi asked in her innocent voice.

"I have never met her in my life. After some days from my birth, she left me and my father. My nursing was fully served by my father. I have only heard a delineation of my beautiful mother from my father."

Hearing this description, expressions of the birds were turned into uneasyness somebody made pityful words for Eaglet. The Sun now had begun to glow very brightly, wind was blowing here and there rapidly, Cataract which was flowing far away from that place, now making his voice louder. As like he was roaring now.

"What is we have before us now?" Sugi asked after some time.

"We have to make Eaglet reside somewhere in the Vihangwanah." said Mooni, "He is all alone."

"That is not possible," Kaka said in his harsh voice, "We can not keep any stranger bird in this forest, namely the Vihangwanah."

Instantly everybody were gazing towards Kaka. (Everybody turned over thier eyes on Kaka)

"But, this eaglet has lost his father somewhere and he does not have anybody close or intimate except us. We should do someting fom this dear eaglet."Koel intimately said.

"But, we can't do anything for him. He is not a resident of the Vihangwanah and that reason he has no any right to stay at this place for long time or for accomodation." Kaka said, he was looking at Koel with his stern black eyes.

All this conversation brought very serioues silence there. Everybody were looking tense and thinking what would be next?

"We can do one thing we can take away this eaglet to his netive place, on deserted tablelands, where from he came?" Parinda suggested.

"That is not possible." Kite spoke with came closer to Parinda, his voice was very calm, "The Eagles can make their fly very long and far away dinstance besides they have the great power in their wings and they can complete about thousands miles journey in the one day. That reason they can easily go all the way. Other hand, this eaglet is still too small to remember the way which he travelled before two nights ago, that was night over then and among us no one so powerful who make way of Eaglet's region or tablelands, with holding him in his claws. This is not even possible to me."

All birds (including two littile animals) nodded their head affirmative on this expalnation of Kite.

"So, what we can do now?" Safeda asked, "It is not possible for him to stay with us for long time."

"Friends, I think that, the father of Eaglet will have gone for hunt and therefore he might have got late." Bagga said and moved his long neck, "He must come by to night."

"Bagga may be right." Kaka seeming self satisfied on the account of Bagga.

"Yes, it is good surmise." Sona hooted, he was moving his yellow eyes. Eaglet brought himself more close to Bagga.

"Because, if his father had gone to somewhere else, he would have told about that to Eaglet and therefore, we have no need to worry. He will come soon at the Vihangwanah with some hunt with him."

"But, what he will do untill his father come back?" Kaka opened his mouth and asked."

"He will stay with somebody in his tree-hole, till his father does not come." Lark put his point.

"This is not possible Lark. The law of the Vihangwanah does not allow this type of interigue." Kaka said and sternly looked at Lark. His voice had suddenly become thorny. "There is needed to be everybird and animals must be consented upon this condition otherwise, this would be disobidence of the Laws of the Vihangwanah."

"Okay, who want Eaglet should stay here, do raise yourr either wing into air and -" looking towards Safeda and Gilhary, Lark said, "-animals do stand on their hind legs for the consentment."

After that everybird did fix raise their one wing on air and Gilhary - Safeda stood on their hind legs, as quickly as they were possible.

But Kaka did not raise his either wing and was looking everybody with disgust eyes.

"It is over! There has been made a decision, Kaka you are only one who is not interested in the decision. Which decision has been taken by the committee, allows that Eaglet stay in the Vihangwanah upto the night."

All birds made their wings down respectively and Safeda - Gilhary relaxed on their four legs.

"Let me tell you Lark. This decision could not be the decision of all committee because-" Kaka said seriously, "Every member is not present for this Assembly at the moment and that reason this Assembly could not be called the complete Assembly. Raghu - *(The various coloured parrot)* has not come for today's Assembly. Therefore, this can not be ideal decision and even your judgement could not be supposed to be right and also your decision could not have consented totally because, in the case, any bird is upsent for the meeting of the Assembly then without being complete the Assembly there could not be made any decision. This is the Law of the Vihangwanah."

Again there spread deep and sound silence among the Assembly members.

"You said right, Kaka, but, I can make vote behalf on that bird, who is not present for the meeting, this is also the law of the Vihangwanah (I think, you might have forgotten this one) I am very glad to say that, I also acknowledge the decision of the rest Assembly." Lark said after raised his one wing.

"Okay, then. The great judgement has been approved in the Assembly here, but I can not accept this type approvel. So, I am not able to stay here for a moment." After that, Kaka spread his black wings and leaped upward to the sky. Sometime after, Kaka disappeared somewhere and left some specks of dust behind him.

Everybody looked to Kaka, but before anyone could stop him he made his way through the number of green trees. Then Lark said, "Now we have to make some preparation about Eaglet's residence. Now tell me, who is interested to take Eaglet to his tree-hole?"

At that moment every bird made their one wing rise upon air, except Sona, Bagga, Safeda, and Gilhary.

"I would have liked to take this innocent eaglet to my land - hole but, I am an animal, not a bird." Safeda said with stiffled his moustache.

"But, I think it would be better that Eaglet make his decision where he wants to stay and also with whom before, we take some decision about his residence." Mooni came forward two steps and suggested then, he asked to Eaglet, "What is your opinion eaglet? Where would you like to stay and also with whom?"

"I will stay with Bagga." Eaglet annouced.

"NO... No." Bagga receded his footsteps, "It is not possible you can't stay with me, any way."

"But, you are like my father indeed, very closely." Eaglet said slightly.

"No. No. I do not look like anybody in your family or even your entire household indeed."

"But ...."

"No. you can't stay with me."

"OH....... But Bagga? Please tell us the reason, why are you saying "not" to eaglet for residing with you?"-asked by Woodpeck, "Why do you deny to stay with Eaglet."

"You all know that I live my life on the Fig tree near here, on the shore of the river. There is not any nest or tree-hole has not been made for me. I live open on the Fig tree under the big canopy of blue sky. I am a free bird and far from the all restriction of life." Bagga spoke and shown his wing towards the direction of Fig tree near the river.

"It is right but this is a matter of an only some time of day and night only. Then what is a problem?" Robin asked in tone of urging.

"Why do you not understand? You also know that I have no protection with me." Bagga said in sick voice, he was teased, "If there will be some danger, I will easily fly away from the danger. But this eaglet is our responsibility now and he can not fly. It is our truely responsibility to protect him from evry harm untill his father do not take him away from here. That reason he can't stay with me in these two conditions."

On the account of Bagga, Lark nodded positively and birds were seeming like agreed.

"Bagga's opinion is very right." Lark said to everyone, "Dear eaglet, now tell us, where would you like to stay instead with Bagga?"

He once looked to Sona and nodded negatively his head (After looking the big yellow eyes of Sona, he had already rejected every option to stay with Sona.)

"There all will be in vain, if this eaglet stay with me. It is day time and I will sleep now. So, it would be better that anyone from you should take away Eaglet." Sona made an explanation.

"I think, we should take him with us in our tree-hole. It is okay Mooni?" Mahina turned her head to her husband and asked, "We both shall be glad."

Mooni gave his permission with nodding his head.

"It is done then............" Lark spoke in loud voice and then asked to Eaglet, "Are you ready to go with Mahina and Mooni, at there tree-hole."

"Yes, I have no problem. I will go with them."

Now, Lark moved towards other birds (including two animals) and asked then, "If you have some complaint concened about this decision, please lift your one wing upward."

"No.No..... If Mahina is taking away Eaglet with her so, I think there should not be any problem at all." Sugi satisfiedly made remark.

"Yeh... Sugi is right. No one can nurse and watch over Eaglet better than Mahina and Mooni can. They are the best at this work." Chidiya affirmalively said, "They both are kind and I am ready to send Eaglet to Mahina and Mooni."

"We accredite this decision." Gilhary told behalf on everybody.

"Ok then. The stranger eaglet will stay with Mahina and Mooni till tonight all responsibility of Eaglet will also on the Mahina and Mooni. This decision has been approved by whole Assembly. So, I kindly request to every member of the Assembly, to take bid from the Assembly now." Lark said with spreading his wings for flight.

"Stop for a moment Lark, we have a problem in front of us." Mooni said and leaped onwards.

"What is the problem, Mooni?"

"It is ok, that we both (Mooni and Mahina) have taken the responsibility of Eaglet but, he can't fly yet and we are both not as strong as to lift up Eaglet and make our way towards our Palsah tree.

So, how will we manage to take away Eaglet to our tree- hole?" Mooni laid a question in front of all birds.

"Oh God! It is big problem indeed." Koel said, "-and that Palsah tree on where Mahina-Mooni reside, that is far away from here."

"You can not fly a little?" Sona asked to Eaglet after looking Sona, he again made two steps back.

"I have not been taught how to fly. I think, I will for always ramain deprieved from the flying." Eaglet answered sadly.

"Don't worry about that. We shall definitely find out some solution on this problem and then deliver you to tree-hole of Mahina and Mooni." Parinda said passionately, "We have been finding a solution on every problem and every bad situation. Wait a minute dear eaglet! We just find a solution."

"But, which solution, we had found out in past among them, every solution had been made by Kaka or Raghu either. Today, Raghu is not present for the Assembly and Kaka has gone to his way, from the Assembly in anger." Robin remarked and asked. "So, now it is our turm to find out the solution."

"I think, we do not have need to find any solution, because, solution are already present here." Kite spoke confidently.

"Solution? which solution." Sugi asked, she was surprised.

"I and Bagga." Kite answered looking towards Bagga. Now, everybody were taken aback with surprise. Gilhary and Safeda were surprisingly looking to Kite. Their faces were extremely termoiled.

"I and Bagga are the biggest birds and also very weighted, Sona is also another bird who is having terrific power, but he can not fly in day light and that reason me or Bagga, can easily hold Eaglet in our claws and easily take him away at residence of Mahina and Mooni." Kite suggeted, his tone was quite explanatory.

There after many birds flapped their wing as like, it was applause for idea of Kite.

"It is good idea, well done Kite, you have found the great solution after all. Now, tell me who is interested in the travel, which will be made towards the Palsah tree of Mahina-and Mooni with the responsibility of Eaglet you or Bagga? Who can complete the task?" Lark questioned to Kite and Bagga. Then, on this Bagga submissively answered to Lark and the Assembly. "I would have complished this task happily. But, you know that my legs are to long too carry any animal, bird or anything. I can not fly very long with holding something in my legs. My speed is slow and therefore, friend Kite you have to fulfil this task I am sorry about that."

"Don't say sorry mate, I will not be troubled a bit from the task." Kite humbly spoke, "I will get happiness through this work. So, are you ready to come with me or I can say, fly with me?"

Eaglet once looked at the Kite then turned towards Bagga and asked, "Can I really not come with you?"

Bagga lifted up his long legs and reached closer to Eaglet, placed his one white wing on the back of his and said, " Dear eaglet, you have shown so much faith on me that I am very happy at the moment. But, I really upset that I am not as powerful as Kite is or not mighty with my limbs like Kite and that reason, I can not deliver you. This is our wish that you should go with Kite please."

On the Bagga's account, Eaglet nodded and went to Kite within two jumps. "Then. It is fine. Mahina and Mooni you both do fly first then, Kite you will fly with Eaglet and after that, the members of the honourable Assembly will fly respectively." Lark announced with loud voice and bowed his head for selute.

Mahina and Mooni once looked at everybird (including Gilhary and Safeda) and they gave their respect to all birds raising their wings respectfully. After that they both leaped into the cold air and then holding Eaglet in claws, Kite spread his steely wings and next moment he leaped into the sky. Everybody gave good compliments (greetings) to Eaglet in their own manner.

When Kite disappeared on one point after that, everbird did fly away one by one from the place of meeting. Safeda and Gilhary jumped into the grass. Big Banyan tree was shaked by air and the water sound of the river could (anybody) have easily heard.

By now Kite had reached on high into the sky. But, he was not flying speedly, because, he had held Eaglet in his claws therefore; he was flying slowly and carefully. Mahina and Mooni now had gone far from Kite but, his keen and hunting eyes was still chasing to Mahina and Mooni.

Eaglet did not have an experience to flying so high into the sky. By now, he had not been taught how to fly or his father also had not taken him away on so up in the air. He was now observing the natural atmosphere of the Vihangwanah from high. There was still some time to noon but, even then the rays of The Sun were very bright and blazing on from top of the sky, Eaglet was beholding downwards green scenery was seeming like, some type of green carpet and only river of the Vihangwanah seeming like embroidery on that green carpet. Because, the river had made plenty of *zigzag* (snaky) turns and going forward. Her water was being glimmared by The Sun rays. Eaglet was very happy to looking the scenery and he was feeling fresh.

"What I may call you?" Eaglet asked.

"What? What did you say?"

Kite could not hear words of Eaglet because, they were going quite fast. Eaglet repeted the question, "I asked that what could I call you?" Eaglet could not keep open his beak for long time because; the pace of air was very rapid one.

"But why? What happened?" Kite turned another direction because, Mahina and Mooni who, were going (flying) ahead, they also had been turned.

"I was about to ask you a question!" Eaglet said.

"Then ask freely! You may call me, whatever you want to call. It will never be important issue for me." Kite spoke loudly and frankly.

"This Vihangwanah seems big."Eaglet asked, "How big it is?"

"Little eagle! It is not big forest indeed. This is the smallest forest in the world I think. It is the only bird forest?" Kite informed to Eaglet.

"It is strange.There, where we live, is not forest and vegetation." like this place. There is only rocks and barren land everywhere.

"OH! It is great." Kite whispered. He did not know whether he show suprise or get sad.

Very soon the Palsah tree was become visible for eyes on some distance. That was big tree and very broad one. The tallest of the all trees. There were lots of beautiful trees and bushes and shrubs around the Palsah tree. Different types of vines were creeping on aromatic grass and by nearing trees.It was all looking like the Heaven.

Mahina and Mooni landed on of the Palsah tree. This tree had accomodation for them. Where the bough had been joined to the Palsah trunk, there was a hole which had been closed with the wooden swoop. Then in very short time, Kite also rested on the same branch with spread his wings. He made drop Eaglet on one side and then he landed some distance ahead. Eaglet balanced himself and came closer to Mahina and Mooni.

"Thank you so much Kite! You did a great job for us." Mooni said humbly.

"There is no need to say thanks."

It is my duty, Mooni and now bid me," Kite spoke with smile, "Good bye, Mahina." Then he turned to Eaglet, "Little lovely eagle, I am get going now, stay happy and I have a great feeling that your father will come back by tonight."

Then Kite spread his wings and leaped down from the bough. He flapped his wings on air; leaves of the Palsah tree were shuddered with air of Kite's wings.

"Come eaglet! Come in. Here is our residence." Mooni came near to eaglet and said, "We all are going to stay here." He has shown his wing towards the swooped hole which was present at the point of the big bough, where they were standing now.

Mahina went ahead and opened the swoop with help of her wings. Thereafter, swoop opened, Mooni was doing every kind of help to sustain Eaglet. Becasue, Eaglet had never climbed on these types of branches in his life. It was different (the unique) experience for him. But, very easily and soon Eaglet reached to opened swoop of the hole without loosing his balance but once; Mahina helped him to enter inside the hole . It was intentinally carved holes for birds by Woodpeck and it was very strong. Every bird lived in this type of tree holes and it was usually called as tree home. It kept protected every bird from harm. Inside the hole there was a matress made by some rags of cloths and fresh cotton. This was an arragement for sleeping.

"It is our tree-hole though it is not very good but,-" Mooni said to Eaglet, "- It is lovely residence for us." The Sun beams were coming inside from the closed wooden swoop, because, there had been made small holes on the wooden swoop for light.

"Your tree hole is very nice indeed. I have never stayed in this type of hole in my whole life." Eaglet praised the tree hole of Mahina and Mooni. He was siting on the piece of fresh cotton.

"How is your home? Where do you live?"

"My home is not in the tree hole or top of the trees. We live in the caves of Rocky Mountains. There atmosphere is very warm." Eaglet said and suddenly asked. "I am getting hungry; can I have something to eat?"

Mahina and Mooni were taken aback and looked at each other.

"OH God! Today I forgot to get something to eat." Mahina answered, she was looking to Eaglet and Mooni back to back, "Today morning, we had to go there for the Assembly and I did not get time for other work. Even to bring fruits! I go to forest and bring some juicy fruits for us okay?"

Hearing these words of Mahina, Mooni hesitatingly said, "You do not need to go anywhere. You just stay here with our little guest and give him some information about this place. I go quickly and pick up some fresh fruits for us." Mooni said and he opened the closed swoop of the hole. He got out and again pulled off the swoop.

"We eat pollen grains inside of the Palshah (tree) flowers. We like that very much. But, ***June months*** has been started and that reason blossom of that flowers have been ceased therefore,now we bring fruits from other tree of the Vihangwanah." Mahina gave information to Eaglet.

"Meant, where we are still now. Is the tree of Pasalah?" Eaglet asked.

"No. Not the pasalah tree, you have articulated wrongly the name of the tree. That is the Palsah tree, *the tree of the spring season.*" Mahina told Eaglet and smiled.

"I have never seen my mother in my life but, my mind is saying though she is not looking like you. Yet, she will be as lovable as you are." Eaglet wrecked his thought hopefully, Mahina looked glimpse of love in his eyes for instance.

"Definitely eaglet, your mother will be more loveble and caring than me. The mother, who can bear loveble eaglet like you, must be very innocent. I am sure that she will meet you once again in your life." Mahina desirably said and moved her wing on his back for showing affection.

Mooni returned after some time. He brought five red small fruits with him; he had caught one fruit in his beak and two in his each claw. No sooner he closed the wooden swoop and came forward than Mahina made her way towards Mooni hesitately; she kept two overloaded fruits from The Mooni's claw.

"Sorry, I am late, because, this is the season of blossoming of various fruits and I wanted some delicious and the sweetest fruits of the Vihangwanah. Therefore, I had got to go quite away from another part of the forest." Mooni placed two fruits near, which he having had and said, "You have been hungry from long time, you should begin to eat it."

"Ah ... There is some problem. I have never eaten this type of fruits ever. How can I eat it?"

"There is no new about that. I know that you don't have an experience about that, therefore, these fruits are very easy to eat. I have chosen this type of special *"Barry"* for you." Mooni made explanation. "Look here, pock your beak in this fruit and absorb all juice from the fruit. If one fruit is not able to fulfill your hunger, you can take another one. These all for you only."

"Let me show you." Mahina went to one fruit and pearce her beak into the fruit and began drinking the juice from the fruit, looking this, Eaglet made same imitation and drinking the juice from another fruit.

One fruit had been enough to extinguish his hunger.

"What happened? Why you stopped yourself? Has your hunger been satisfied on one fruit only?" Mooni asked.

"Yes, I can not absorb a drop of juice any more." Eaglet said satifactorily.

"Okay. Okay, now have a rest." Mahina said, "You have been awaking from long time."

The morning time had been changed into noon. There were black clouds gathered in the sky. There had been heavy rain in the Vihangwanah from some days. But, yesterdy and today, there was no rain but only cloudy weather all over and therefore, Eaglet cloud be found by birds otherwise, he would havebeen sweeped away by the numerous treams of flowing water.

After that, morning time transformed into the evening very soon. The Sun had been retiring from his busy day's job. (Though there were many clouds in the sky.) But, there was not any strange incident happened in the Vihangwanah yet.

Mahina and Mooni were pacing up and down in their tree-hole desperately. They had been thinking about Eaglet's father from morning. Eaglet was in deep sleep and evening looking like (was) to be over.

"His father is still to come back."Mahina nurvously said, "It is too late"

"I am thinking, somebody would have definitely found some clue about him." Mooni hopefully conveyed his thoughts.

At the very moment, the wooden swoop was banged and Mooni forwarded to open the swoop. He opened; it was Robin who was standing out side of the tree hole. (Doorway.)

"Robin, you are here? What is the matter?"

Robin recovered his wings and said, "The Sun has been seted, has Eaglet's father come back or not?"

Mahina came near to Mooni and looking in Mooni's eyes with the indecative notion, the silent beetween Mahina and Mooni was greatly understood by Robin, he spoke, "Eaglet's father has not returned, Thisis night time now. I have come here because, eaglet's father has not come back yet and This means - " He looked to Mahina and Mooni one after another, his tone was changed into low voice, "- It is the time for another Assembly, So get your way to the big Banyan tree, near the river (where first Assembly was held). I am going to inform other bird -friends, Good night."

Robin flapped his wings and leaped into the twilight. Twilight always presents a question and today's question was one of the important and difficult one. Robin turned back from some distance, he became stable into air with flapping his wings and he said to Mahina and Mooni, "I send Kite to pick up Eaglet." Then having taken a graceful swerved in the air he obscured some where into darkness.

Lot of time had been passed after The Sun setting, only the river of the Vihangwanah babbling steadily and unexpected rain was started that was not heavy but, drizzling rain. It was like shower from the sky. The every drop of the rain falling into the river water and composing a delicate music.

Before, beginning the sprinkling rain, every bird was present under the big banyan tree, where Assembly was to hold. (Only one bird not reached to the spot.) The big Banyan tree was about *Five hundred years old* and one of the oldest tree of the Vihangwanah and as well as an ancient one. The Banyan tree had been spread very vast and that reason, drops of the rain could not be reached to bottom of the Banyan tree, where birds had been gathered. (Assembly was held.). Gilhary had collected dried leaves and branches of the trees and adeptly set fire from them. In the light of the bonefire. The Assembly was to begin. Every member of the Assembly was waiting, who was yet to come. At the moment everybody heard a flapping sound of wings and Raghu *(The various coloured parrot)* admitted himself among, the gathering birds, with sprinkling drops of the rain water on them.

"Sorry ! Sorry ! The way could not see clearly because, rain and I had gone out of the Vihangwanah for some of work. Therefore, I got quite late." Raghu apologised in his firm voice, "Lark, I am sorry for having late."

"There is no need to say sorry. Because, Assembly is yet to begin it"s work."

Lark humbly spoke, "Okay, now I give you an idea about why this Assembly is being held-"

"Do not tell me circumstances of the Assembly (any information about the meeting) Because, I have been given all the information. This little white eaglet is the subject of this Assembly and we all have been gathered here for the decision." Raghu pointed out his one wing towards Eaglet and said.

("Raghu always knows everything." Robin said in the ear of Parinda, he nodded.) Along with eyes of Mahina and Mooni, every bird moved their eyes on Eaglet. Eaglet made his way closer to Mooni after looking big and yellow eyes of Sona staring at him. (Really Sona was looking at eaglet but not with fierce look but amazed one.)

The little bonefire was blazing in yellow and red and brown coloures. Dried levels were burning with wicked sound of sparkling. There was drizzling of rain out side of the branches of the big Banyan tree although, the bonefire had been blazing grimly.

"We are wasting our time on Eaglet. There was no need of the Assembly. Because, this eaglet has not been come from any of us and he is not an inhabitant of the Vihangwanah. It is our wasted time that we came here from long distance. No decision can be taken in this Assembly. So it is in vain indeed." Kaka spoke in his black voice. On which tree he lived that was far away from the spot of the Assembly. From the beginning he had been behaving hard-hertedly and harshly with Eaglet. He used to talk very scathingly (virulently) about Eaglet.

Kaka's talk did spread sound silence among birds only sound which could be heard, was the sound of rain dropps which were falling in the river water.

"Kaka, it is an elget, the small offspring and now he has been the part of the Vihangwanah." Bagga said respectfully.

"He can not be part of the Vihangwanah becasue, he is not a offspring of any of us. He does not have this hereditary right or-" Kaka once glanced at Safeda and Gilhary and continued his talk. "- He is not belong to any little animal and this creed of the bird namely the Eagle and in that white eagle is rare one and does not find by our surrounding also, we do not know how this eaglet did get come here? I am firm that he might be a spy."

"This all conversation had been made in the moring and we had reached at this conclusion that if eaglet's father did not come back till night then we were to hold an Assembly and discuss about, what will have to do with Eaglet." Sona told, looking his yellow eyes, Eaglet again pulled back his footsteps.

"That's mean his father was not inerested look after him therefore, he abondoned Eaglet at this strange place, means at the Vihangwanah. It is visible like The Sun light, his father left him ...."

Mooni came forward after hearing this and spoke. "Believe me Kaka, I do not think that any bird will ever abondon his offspring to this type of unknown forest. Because this is not the cult of birds. Every bird loves his offspring and love is a nature of birds and after that this eaglet belonged to rocky mountain and stony regions. That is far from here. I am thinking that area is about thousands miles from here and no bird will do so long journey of this green part only to leave their young one alone. So, there is not a possibility that this eaglet had been abondoned. We are not the Humans who leave their young alone."

"Yes, It is right. This weaked deed could not be done by any bird or animal we hate this type of treatment. We all know that very well." Safeda revealed his feelings.

The rain had been slowed down and drops sound, which falling in the river water was heard slowly. But, Gilhary was doing her job gradually, she was still putting dried branches and leaves into the bonefire (For give warmness and light to The Assembly members.

"Now, I am going to begin conversation of the respected Assembly. We can't wait for Eaglet's father any more, this is night time and which time we had expected to return his father that has been over now. So, his father will come back or not it is un certain question. So, our proccedings should begin now. "

"But, I thought that my father would come back very soon to pick up me." Eaglet said and casted his brown eyes on every bird (including two animals) except Sona one, "He will never leave me alone."

On this point, the heart breaking silence spread again among whole Assembly. Mahina made his way towards Eaglet and said, "Dear eaglet, perhaps your father misled the way and he did not find the way of the Vihangwanah. Therefore, he might be late. Will you stay here till that time with us?" She placed her wing on back of Eaglet.

"Ka....... Kasss Kass ..... Kow .... Kak -" Kaka said something in his language "It is called "hopeful disguise" His father had been come back, If he would have been alive." His tone was exeptionally hateful.

"Kaka . .... If you are going to speak further like this in front of Eaglet. It would be better to close your black mouth next time." after said this, Raghu leaped from his place and came near to Kaka.

Raghu was about two times bigger than Kaka and one time bigger than Kite therefore, Kaka used to talk very controlable in front of Raghu.

Hearing this poignant words from Raghu, Kaka moved from one side and stood in dark corner from Raghu. Raghu was still staring at Kaka.

"Now, tell me, what decision we have to take about Eaglet first, Then I will make my judgement after hearing your point." Lark said franckly. He was standing in front of the bonefire, head to head with Raghu. Which round was made by birds and small animals for standing, Raghu and Lark was standing at the center of that circle.

"This type of "Black question" had never been in front of us. It is like a unsolved riddle for the Vihangwanah." Dove said, he was being glimmered Blue and Brown in the blazing -fire of the bonefire.

"We can leave Eaglet some other part of this area on any another forest." Parinda spoke. Suddenly, every eye of the Assembly turned towards Parinda. Having noticed that, he used his next words very carefully-, "If any one of you has no objection."

"It could not be accepted." Gilhary spoke at first time, She was moving his fairy tail (she was standing on his hind legs and with the help of front clow (hands) she was putting dried things into the bonefire)," Anybody from among us, can not take this type of decision and If everybody has taken this type of decision. I would be stand against it and do protest for Eaglet."

Many birds shook their heads positively as like they were accented on Gilhary's explanation. Everybody was trying to rainforce the statement of Gilhary. But, Kaka nodded his head negative and slightly uttered some disgust words but, no one did not care of them. Debate went ahead when, Safeda spoke in his weak voice. As like he was afraid to Kaka, as thinking that Kaka would leap on him if he heard his words. "I comptelely vindicate to Gilhary's statement."

"Thank you Safeda."

"We can not leave Eaglet alone because, he is not enough mature and he can not live without anyone's support yet." After the words of Safeda, affection and carring feeling spread among the gathered birds around there.

"We can not leave Eaglet alone here or any where because, this is not only the answer to concerned about this Assembly." Sona spoke. "What is ahead of us?"

"What is ahead? But nothing. I think we let Eaglet stay here with us in the Vihangwanah and rear him lovingly." Bagga suggested, came forward two steps from his place. When the blazing light of the Bornefire fallen on him, his white coloured body was began to glimmering in golden colour and he appeared like the Magical - Golden - Globe.

"It is not possible." a rude voice came from another side, No bird had disagreement about, whose voice was that, Kaka again came at the center of gathered birds and his oratory was feeling like an outburst of the valcano. "This eaglet can not stay here, at the Vihangwanah, If you gathered birds and -" He casted his hateful sight on Safeda and Gilhary, "- animals are thinking like this, then I could have to say that, This is a foolish thinking, really idiocy-"

"You can not use these types of abusive words here Kaka, and it is not right to use these words on your comrades. This rule of our Assembly you have known -" Lark said in strict tone, he was angrily looking to Kaka; But Kaka used his oratory in spectaculating manner. "I know every rule and law and regulation of the Vihangwanah and honourable Assembly also." He used his words carefully, "- and I did not use any contemptible word on my any comrade, who has been gathered here, but, I used it for their respective decision, which they have taken. So, there is no question about violating any rule of the Assembly or disrespect any comrade here."

The drizzling of rain had been stopped now and except babbling sound of the river water, there was no other sound.

"We know that you had not used those words for us or you did not use those deliberately too. But which decision we have taken here that you are thinking abusive, Kaka?" Gilhary questioned, she was offended by the words of Kaka.

"Because, no one could stay or live here, coming from abroad and it could not be accepted by any inhabitants of the Vihangwanah. This is one of the most important rule of the Vihangwanah and it is rule *No.12*." Kaka was looking towards Eaglet and said ahead scornfully, "If you did not forget the rules-"

"I don't think, anybody in the Assembly could have forgotten the rules. I suppose that, everyone knows every minor law of the Vihangwanah." Kite said, and came closer to Kaka. He was constantly staring in black eyes of Kaka, "Because, some birds among us who are present here, their honourable ancestors also lived here and these all rules and laws of the Vihangwanah had been made by them."

Having heard this, Kaka came more close to Kite, if he had made one more step ahead, he he could have easily touched his beak to Kite's and spoke in his poisonous voice, "My ancestors also had been the part of hte Vihangwanah they staked their lives and minds for the making of the rules and the law's of this forest. They burnt their blood for the security of the Vihangwanah. But, I have to say with regret that the hard working of our ancestors as well as their valuable lives are being wasted here. Because, some birds and animals are now forggeting the rules of the Vihangwanah."

"- It is totally wrong because-" Bagga furiously went on, "- which ancestors had made the laws of our forest, in that committee five types of birds were involved and their generations are also now present here at the moment. My own ancestor had been part of that law committee, their Raghu's ancestor, your ancestors and some other bird's ancestors had been present there that time and they worked hard for the rainforcement of the Vihangwanah. Kaka, which hard work had been done by your ancestors, same that type of hard work done by every bird of the committee. Those efforts only were made for walfare of our forest and for their following (upcoming) generations. Those laws had been made for the sake of the Vihangwanah. But, even then how can you say that we are going to forget the laws of the

Vihangwanah, even after you know better that our ances tors also had halped for making these laws."

"Because-" Kaka casted his black signt on every bird and two little animals, "- Everyone is using here the language of the permanent resident or accomodation of Eaglet without thinking about the the respected laws of the Vihangwanah. Therefore, I want to say that, no other animal or any bird can be the life time part of the Vihangwanah. Only the inhabitant birds will be the part of the forest till last. So, there is no question about the staying of Eaglet here it can not be granted otherwise, it will be vaolation of rule no.12."

At this point Lark, who was standing at the centre, was looking very desturbed. Rain was stopped and remaning drops of the water on tree leaves now sliping down from the leaves from trees and falling into the river water or standing water near. Every sliping drop was taking some time to drip and that time was very hard to pass away for the gathared birds.(Assembly members.)

"But, these laws and rules when having been made, that time those inventor of the rules and laws should have thought more about this type of emotional or delicate situation. They ought to have found the exact solution on it. We were not in the world when these types of laws were made." Koel spoke in her sweet voice.

"Look it, the ancestors thought on it or not it is we don't know. But which laws they had made they are very exact and right." Kaka said confidently "And the laws of Vihangwanah are not written they are just oral or unwritten." (But some have been written also.)

"If everyone respects to the laws of the Vihangwanah so we also do our job under the right of the laws." Sugi suggested. But she also was hesitated.

"If we go with out of the rules and laws then we should have to leave this eaglet on the other place or another forest-." Kaka said, moving his eyes on everyone, "- and this type of execution will not do any harm to our rules and laws."

"Enough is enough Kaka." snddenly Mahina spoke in domanating tone, "I know that you have the great knowledge of every kind of laws and rules. You are proud on them and you haev been also a great philosopher and student of this laws. But, let your mind notice that there is the great word which can dominate your laws and rules. The word is *"compensation toward birds"* means *"love for birds"* It is a relation of affection and emotion. If your laws do not get protection to offspring and other birds so your law is only the unaninated laws and rules and I don't think that your law ever will have saved anybody or any live either. If your law had been so powerful, so it would have saved my son and he could have been alive today with us and every bird of the Vihangwanah will be living matromonial (conjugal) life..... happy life." Mahina's words were like the keen arrows and in her eyes gathered the tears of sorrow. These tears were glimering in the blazing of bonefire and appearing like the precious pearls. "I know only that this eaglet has fallen into danger and If we are, so many comrade birds are present here and even then this eaglet will have to lead an alone life. So, I say that, everybody of us should regard himself as the "cold hearted" and lead life as it is and If this Assembly is taking the decision that Eaglet should lead the alone life in some other forest then me and my husband Mooni will go with him Because, If you negleat any little or alone live (bird) only for sake and respect of your laws then I say that your life is not life but only the dead skeleton of the life and laws."

Mooni came ahead to console Mahina after she completed her talk.

"Ttalk of the Mahina is very right. Eaglet will not go anywhere from here. It is my firm decision." Sugi spoke and placed her wing on the back of Mahina.

"I also think so." Koel said pussionately.

"I also agreed with the decision." Woodpeck raised up his one wing on the air and said.

The Safeda and Gilhary stood their two legs for showing their consentment. "okay.. If your decision take intomind then. There is no issue to disaggrement on-" Lark was speaking but, his speak was disconnected by Kaka and he spoke in his angree voice, "what is it? This type of consetment is openely abusement of the Assembly and also the laws of the Vihangwanah and this is also the disrespect of my ancestors, it is not only dishonour of my ancestors but also the dishonour of your ance-"

"Kaka- " Raghu shouted so furiously that Kaka became silent and went two steps back, "Look Kaka, I know that your ancestors had been the part of real law Assembly in the Vihangwanah. But, I would like to make remember again, that our ancestors also had been part of that Assembly. In that Assembly Sona's grand father and also Bagga's grandfather were the oldest birds and today Sona and Bagga the oldest birds among us and I feel very proud to saying that grandfather of Sona had done very hard labour for making the laws. Because, Sona's species is only species among us who can keep awake through the whole night and Sona's grandfather used to wake through the night and seach of the various laws and rules that time. Then in the day time he set up the ideology of that laws and rules before the Old Assembly. Therefore, Sona has the great responsibility of the cultivation of the laws of Vihangwanah, where Sona lives at this time. That tree-hole on the *"Khairrah tree."* is very ancient and some generations of the Sona had lived their. Inside of that tree-hole."

"There you can see some inscription, that inscription are the laws and rules of the Vihangwanah and that had been carved there by grandfather of Sona. Therefore, you are not only a bird who concerned with the committee of the laws of the Vihangwanah. Kaka, here is being one bird who has great knowledge of laws more than you and me and all of us and he is *Sona* only. So, what does Sona thinks at the time is more important than our feeling or conversation. We should show some respect towards the opinion of Sona." then Raghu turned to Lark (and said), "Lark, I am sorry, I talked in very high voice inded in the Assembly. I honour this Assembly with my heart and I also say sorry to Kaka." Raghu went one side and stood there silently.

But, Kaka was not free bird to easily remit anyone his feelings were very badly affronted with the talk of Raghu who said that Sona had the great knowledge about every thing and laws. But he did not say anything because, there was pin dropped silent and everyone was looking at Sona, who had been standing by the side of Bagga.

"I am very glad and thank to Respectable president of the Assembly, Lark who gave me a chance to deliver my thoughts in the Assembly, in front of my mates," Sona said with bowing his head down and his voice was very humble, at this point Lark also bowed his head towards Sona. But Eaglet got closer to Mooni because, he had seen yellow and Big eyes of Sona, "We all birds and animals have the part of the Assembly and everyone has privilege and right to deliver their deliberation or opinion. In the ancient rules and laws, there was great hard work had been done by my respected grandfather for the Assembly, I think it is not correct because every bird (ancient) had taken the same labour for making stronger the laws of the Vihangwanah every bird had helped a lot and that reason everyone was equal for the law committee. Those laws are alive still today and will till live very last moment of the Vihangwanah or bird life. But, when, the laws are thought about the companssation of the birds, that time, we have to notice the comments of Mahina and Mooni and I aslo think that is right on at this moment that there is not question about breaking of laws or abusement or violation of the rules but, the life of the alone bird is more important. Therefore. I can understand the relation between Eaglet and Mahina - Mooni and So, I take decision with the respect of my common membership of the Assembly that I agreed with the decision or view of Mahina and Mooni. Eaglet should live with us in the Vihangwanah."

At the very moment, all birds expressed their happiness with flapping of wings even Raghu and Lark also flapped their wings. It heard like the applause Sona said thanks to everybody and did bent his head for showing the selutation for everybody.

"I aslo take the side of Sona's conviction because, we are intimate friends for each other, and also our great ancestors were part of the great Assembly of the laws." Bagga said, looking towards Sona and touched his wing to each other. (They were smiling and looking like making shakehand to each other.)

"Thank Bagga and Sona." Lark humbly spoke. He was standing near the trunk of the Abhata tree (and speaking ahead), " Now, who is agreed with The Mooni-Mahina, Bagga and Sona's view, please raise their wing in air and which animal-"

"-We are already consented with them, and you can consider our accent on their respectable decision." Hearing the incomplete the talk of Lark, Safeda clarified his decision looking towards Gilhary. She also nodded in affermative.

On the announcement of Lark every birds raised their one wing still in air and shown their agreement.

"Thank you, you can bring your wings down" Lark said looking of everybody, "So, now, this eaglet will be the part of the Vihangwanah to very last of his life. I am Lark, the president of the Assembly, annouce that Eaglet will live in this forest namely the Vihangwanah forever. This consentment of the respected Assembly and everybird-" He casted a sight on Kaka, who had about disappeared in one gloomy corner because, of his black colour, "-is being passed (agreed) by me and this will be the final decision of the Assembly."

Everybird was about to celebrate their joy but suddenly-

"-Let damn this type of decisions and agreements." Kaka shouted so furiously that His macabre voice began to feel more macabre. Hearing the voice everybody shuddered with fear and horror then, they realised that the voice belonged to Kaka.

"You all at once time were friend of mine and I was the respected president of this Assembly then, before some weeks you elected Lark on the presidentship instead of me. But I did not mind that or I did not make regret. But, today only for an offspring or Eaglet you have broken the rules of the Vihangwanah and gone against me also. yet, It is hard for me to believe your opinion and agreement."

"Listen Kaka -" Woodpeack was speaking sliently but, Kaka flicked off his talk and said further on, "you don't dare to speak with me." His voice was overflowing with rage and horror. Woodpeak became very sad to hearing this and put down his head.

"Kaka, you have belied to our decision." Mooni came ahead and did speak, "we have not gone against to you ever and not going at the moment or in the future also, other hand you are going oppisite to us at the moment."

"- And untill there is a question of breaking the laws of the Vihangwanah. I think (that) we have not broken any rule for any cheaper reason and I am feeling -" Mahina was compensately saying, "Having taken this type of decision we might have seluted to our great ancestors and their honourable spirits wherever they are, as we suppose after death we go on the charming *"Ameya parbata"* which is alike the Paradise for us perhapsour ancestor might be watching us from there and praising us as well.

(Yes it is right because, we have realised the cost of loving realation and we have honoured it." Woodpeck whispered.)

"What are you saying that is right only for listen? But, think about the present condition indeed. For all of us this is really very serious and hard time notice it (mind it). From how long we have been sacrifising for secure us. Among us, only a pair having married at the moment. Between them Koel having been married even then she in she lives alone. There is only couple here, who is leading successful life, Mahina and Mooni and that is the only couple in the Vihangwanah everybody conscious about the present condition I know that. But, we are leading Eaglet into danger with taking the risponsibility of him. Give attention on the fact. I did not agree with your decision and the Assembly decision till yet."

"So, your thinking has not been changed yet then," Raghu spoke. He was looking very different coloured in the reducing flames of the bonefire, "It is our responsibility now, to protect his life. We can sacrifice our present lives for securing his future and protect him from every ghastly situation in his life. It is only duty to us now onwords you can fulfill your life with lift up responsibility of Eaglet along with us."

Kaka nodded his head and uttered a damn word and said, "If you want to sacrifice your life for sake of the useless and worthless eaglet then sacrifice your life happily but, keep not any hope from me. My life is not as useless as any worthless eaglet. I wish that you will send me a message or notice for next Assembly. The night has enough dark and it is too late and my tree - hole is far from here so, I say adieu to this Assembly and you and take bid from the Assembly. May God bless you with comfortable night and enough good brain. Good bye and Good night." Having casted a black sight on everyone and flyed into air with flapped his wings, he stopped for moment and casted hateful sight on Eaglet, then he turned away very easily in the air and obscured into the darkness some where far from the spot of meeting.

As Kaka gone from there, It was feeling that he pulled away with him all the rapture and enthusiasm of the Assembly. After he gone even then there was stress atmosphere everywhere in the birds and the Assembly.

"Kaka's point was not totally wrong one." Sona said in calm voice after some time. He was looking at that place where Kaka had stood before some time.

"But, you can not say that he was totally right, Sona." Bagga unttered looking at Sona.

"Now decision has been consented and it is last decision. Once we have taken decision then we should stay firm on that. We can not give our steps back." Sugi said.

"Listen me Sugi, I do not think that anybody will pull back his legs from this decision. Because, we have got hope for live life more happily and enthusiasmly from this eaglet. Untill now we just live because living was restriction for us. But now, we have more great reason to live ahead." Parinda spoke with flapping his wings as he had just come inside from the rain, "-we shall live for great opportunity indeed and if you ask me I say that it is good news for us."

On this point Robin came front and said gladly "Yes, Parinda it is rigth. How many years after - a little live- has admitted among us and to protect his life is the aim of our life. It is ordeal for us. In which serious atmosphere we were living that, had been very monotonus for us. But now, our live will be hopeful very soon."

Robin's talk spread there motivation among bird circle.

"But, I have still a question in my mind." Dove spoke very uneasily, "What will happen if father of Eaglet come back today or tomorrow?"

After this question again all hopes faded away from that place. It seemed like somebody pulled away that hopes and spirit and vitality.

"If Eaglet's father comes here back again, then, we shall send him away with his father." Mahina was looking to everybody and said, "Finally blood relation is a blood realation and we are not relatives of Eaglet with blood that reason, we can not take the place of his father or mother either."

"Yes it is right point Mahina! But, untill Eaglet will live here, the decision of the Assembly will remain stable as Eaglet will be the resident of the Vihangwanah for ever. But there is a question ahead me." Lark said determinationly, "Who will nurse Eaglet?"

"I would not believe. If anyone told me that so many questions would be put in front of us in today's Assembly indeed." Kite whispered in Koel's ear and she nodded affirmatively.

"Whenever we are asked the question about care and nursing there only couple, who comes in front of our eyes-" Gilhary said, she was still putting dried leaves, branches, hay in the bonefire to keep it afire steady , "-Mahina and Mooni. They have been rearing Eaglet since the morning and Eaglet also has been inhabited to Mahina and Mooni. Therefore, I say that it would be better if Eaglet stay with Mahina and Mooni as we know that no one can look after Eaglet better than Mahina and Mooni. They are the best."

Now everyone turned their eyes to Mahina and Mooni. But Mahina and Mooni were looking to each other very sentimently and meditatingly as like they were convassing to each other through their eyes. They did not say a word. Then Raghu asked question them, "What happened Mahina and Mooni? What Gilhari said some time ago have you consented on that or not? What is your opinion about Eaglet? (Have you accepted it or not)? "

On the point Mooni said passionately, "which belief you all have kept on us, that is very hopeful and we both thank to you. We know Eaglet very well now and I think he also became friendly with us. We have been bonded with each other through an unidentified relation. We do not have any problem to look after Eaglet. Where we shall beglad and please. But, at last there comes the point of nursing, education and protection, among these, we can not give him anything except *love*. Because, this is an eaglet and we are the birds of very low race. At the time, the Vihangwanah is occupied with very serious and mysterious danger. We all know that we both are not so strong to proetect and save Eaglet, in the case any danger fallen on him. Then, there is another big problem that we don't have any experience, how to train Eaglet and how to coach him and we are not able to educate him probably so, that reason we dare not to protect or rear Eaglet."

"Listen to me Mahina and Mooni. Except you no one is here more experienced enough in this subject. You are the only here whocan take the responsibility of Eaglet." Lark spoke and he looked to surrounding birds and the two little animals, "If anybody from you wants to take the responsibility of Eaglet, please come two steps ahead."

But no one did come ahead because everybody was unadepted in this subject there execpt, Mahina and Mooni.

"Can I not stay with this uncle?" Eaglet asked a question with showing his wing towards Bagga. Everybody looked at Bagga but, Bagga did think some time and made his way close to Eaglet and told him with care, " Dear eaglet, I would have liked to stay you with me. But I have no tree-hole like other birds and Mahina Mooni's home. I live on branches of the *Fig tree* little distance from here. Rain falls horribly there and you will get wet. There feel the great chill-cold which can not be endured by you. You can not come with me for next some days. But, with whom you want to stay except me?"

Eaglet was seeming some more satisfied and he aswered, "-Then I-" His head moved towards Mahina and Mooni, "-will stay with them, untill my father does not return."

Having heard these words from Eaglet, Hearts of the birds and animals were filled with kindness. But, everbody was seeming enough safisfied with the own decision of Eaglet. (He himself told his decision to Assembly that he would stay with Mahina and Mooni.)

"Ok then. I proclaim that Eaglet will live to Mahina and Mooni till last of his life in case his father not return." Lark declared.

"But, Lark -" Mooni tried to tell something. But Lark did not listen his word and spoke ahead, "Do not take any tension about that, Mooni and Mahina. You only keep Eaglet in your supervision. Do not think that he is only your responsibility; Eaglet is the responsibility of all us. Therefore, in every day and night two birds will keep watch on the *Palsah tree* of Mahina and Mooni's. I will make the timetable of it very soon and send to you through Robin in some days. Then, Sona and Kite you both are the great Fighters and this is your responsibility, That you will teach Eaglet every minor and major tactic of the Fighting and also give him a knowledge of flying and overwitting on danger and how to come out safe and sound from the danger. Untill I will think more and more take some knowledge how to teach and make him a bird like an eagle and then tell you about the next plan. Then Parinda, sefeda and Woodpeck you will convey any strange news or information of any bird. You have been doing this work from many years but now the importance of that work has been increased and I know you are the best spy. I have or the Vihangwanah experienced ever. It is time to do more hard work for all of us."

Safeda, Parinda and woodpekk noddad their head respectively for consentment.

"do Have you still any problem or worry?" Raghu asked to Mahina and Mooni.

"NO. Now, there is not any problem. We are become happy and thank to everybody who presented here. You have stood powerfully behind us." Mahina said and two tears dropps abruptly fallen down which were glimmering from long time in her eyes.

"Mahina, we all have stood for each other and this is our power we always have been helping to each other. That reason your happiness is our happiness." Raghu -Various coloured parrot said with smile.

"This is long night enough now. It is very late. It is the time for us to leave now." Lark held his eyes on everyone and said, "-And rain also been stopped. I again hand over responsibilty of take away Eaglet at Mahina and Mooni's tree hole on Kite. Kite you have to take away Eaglet to Mahina and Mooni's tree hole on the Palsah tree and I also proclaim that this is the conclusion of the Assembly....our respected Assembly of the Vihangwanah and thank to Every member to give their help, mind and time for the Assembly thank you."

At the very moment, in darkness, everybird was flying towards his tree-hole rspectively. When all birds were completely vanished from there, only the bonefire which had been ablazed some time ago. Now that was extingnished but, remaining ember of bonefire was blazing after some interval of time and some blaze were still raising their heads from the ember -yellow and brown and red.

****

SECOND

The morning of the next day was very fresh. Eaglet had awoken from his deep sleep. Mahina and Mooni had brought delicious fruits for Eaglet some time ago and he had eaten them very likely. But, noon was not fresh enough because, that afternoon Black clouds had been gathered in the sky and after that there fallen heavy rain. Therefore, the only river of the Vihangwanah has been flowing very rapidly and furiously, her water raised very high the waves touched to the shore and the only Fig tree was standing, on the shore, come into danger and therefore, Bagga left his residence and had to shalter on a elegant tree for long time. But, after some time rain stopped. That rain was one of the heaviest rain of the Vihangwanah. When rain was stopped Bagga again went back to the Fig tree. But, when he reached there, he did not get anything without fustration there. Beacause, the water of the river was flowing spidily around the Fig tree and seeming like that at any moment the tree will sweep away with the muddy water. Therefore, Bagga thaught about his best friend and his best friend's tree hole. So, however, he could get shelter tonight and he also will not get sickness or fever. Bagga's best friend had a another great quality that he would not sleep at night and his residence was very near to Bagga's Fig tree.

When Bagga, after some time, reached near '*the khairrah*' tree, he saw that in that place, there was not much standing water therefore, the trees were remained secured from every harm by flowing water. Even then, there was everywhere Black dark darkness but, Bagga surmised the situation, on the base of his hearing power.

Bagga did not have any need to knock on the wooden swoop. Because, Sona was still awaking and the wooden swoop was also kept open.

"Sona, are you in?" Bagga called out, because, he could not see inside, there was darkness inside the hole. He only guessed.

"Who .....? Bagga you are! At this time! Come in! Come in!" Sona reached to open swoop entrance of hole. He sustained his wings for help to Bagga, Who could only see the big yellow eyes of Sona, "How did you get so wet?" he asked.

"What I tell you Sona! The rain was falling so, heavily that the river is flowing with shore to shore, noisely. I thought that rain would stop soon. But, rain was heavily falling and falling and therefore the lavel of water were rising and rising to the dangerous point. My Fig tree did come into danger and I had to come to you for shelter."

"It was to happen one day. I have told you about thousands time that you should carve the tree hole from Woodpeck for you. But, you never listened to me. This is not good to stay open on the tree. Bagga, any danger can find you! (You could be fallen in danger one day.)." Sona made lecture for Bagga.

"You are right Sona. I should have asked Raghu or woodepeck for my tree-hole already But, Ok now, after somedays I will make a tree-hole for me."

"- Okay then, after that you will have not to defeat before the natural powers and you will not to need to shelter in the other birds - or mine tree-hole. I would think that it is your second time to shelter in my tree-hole, isn't it?" Sona asked suddenly.

"Ah ...... No", After kept thinking for moment Bagga said, "It is my third time indeed, But I am still happy to shelter in your home, that mean, I can chat with you for long time with the course of this stay."

"Yes, that is the great advantage for us." Sona smilily said, "Ok have you got some information about who will, when, where give Eaglet training about all things? And who will watch over on Mahina and Mooni's Palsah tree."

"No, I do not know about that." Bagga said, He knew that, he was not able to look in darknees, but Sona could easily look everything. Bagga was trying to look to Sona, and answered in that direction.

"Today, from the morning, rain has been rampaging everywhere that reason, Lark might have not got time for manage timetable for us. Perhaps, He will not able to make timetable from only his base therefore, he will have to consult with anybody. May be this type of problem would be in front of Lark. Then, there was not possibility to work over the timetable today. Because of rain, there had been struggle for bread and butter at the time."

"I think then you must have not eaten anything?" Sona questioned.

"Yes, I had gone out of from my place and I got little late to return and therefore, after then rain was started so heavily, I could not do anything for myself."

"OKAY. It is goodness that I had gone to hunt on previous night and brought some fishes for me. One have still with me you can eat that one." Sona made his way another part of his tree- hole and he got one fish holding in his beak and placed it by the legs of Bagga.

Saying "*thank you*", In the little time, he finished it off. When Bagga was eating a fish, in course of that time Sona kept silent.

"How can we nurse that eaglet? He is the offspring of the eagle and his creed also very high - he has great creed tradition behind him. So, how we, the birds of lower race, can manage to teach him everything, for His up-coming life?" Sona asked thoughtfully.

"That is also riddle for me, Sona. We all are very small birds and we also are not skilled in that, which is the bloodly cult of the egale. Their life style is also different," Bagga made an account, "There is a question that to where from where we will have to teach him."

"Yes, It is a point, but I think that Lark will be thinking about it and Raghu also help him on that matter and find out the way. Because, they both have the great knowledge about everything perhaps, they will guide us. About all education of Eaglet?"

After that there spread silence for a moment. That course of the silence was being disturbed by the slipping drops of rain-water from the leaves of the surrounding trees and peculiar sounds of the rain frogs.

"The tomorrow's morning, perhaps, will give the answer of every question. But, the protection of Eaglet is the greatest issue for every bird friend. This question is standing before us like the Himalayah."

"That is may be right but, I have the worry of tomorrow because of that I have been weted heavily and If I am not wrong about, I may have been cold and fever." Bagga worringly said "Tomorrow I first shall go to Dove for treatment If-"

"-If there will be no rain like today's." Sona completed his sentence with laugh.

Next morning, The Sun aroused slowly in the morning and life of the Vihangwanah was begun. But this morning was unusual morning for every resident of the Vihangwanah. Eaglet could not get out from the tree-hole where he living with Mahina and Mooni. Therefore, he had come out and siting on the front branch looking the impact of rain, which had been fallen last night. On every leaves, drops of rain were shining like sliver- pearls and diamonds. Scenery like this he had never seen in his little life. Sometime after Mooni came out from the tree hole and stood near Eaglet.

"It is better and fresh atmosphere comparing to yesterday." Mooni took long breath and spoke.

"The atmosphere of *that night* was also cloudy and stormy too." Eaglet said and glanced at Mooni.

"On which night?"

"Which night I had been reached here with my father. That night was storny and cloudy because, my father was struggling for flying."

"You have not told anything partaining about it to any bird why did you not tell at that very time?"

"I don't know, I remembered that night when I looked this atmosphere and stormy rain. And I now remembered another thing - Which I have to tell you." Eaglet made moved to Mooni and said. He was serious.

- "which thing?"

"In That night, when my eyes opened for instance in my sleep, that time I saw some bird, who was standing by me. But, I don't recongise which type of bird that was?"

Having heard this, Mooni's heart burned with something.

"How was looking that bird, how big was he?" Mooni reached very close to eaglet and asked impationatly.

"I also do not know that, I was in sound sleep that time and there was very darkness around me. That reason I only could see his shape only."

Mooni was thinking now and made question, "Perhaps that might be your father?"

"I do not have idea about that, but I can definitely tell that my father is not so small in shape. That bird was not big as my father is."

Now, Mooni's mind was full with the storm of questions. Who was that bird, which stood by the side of Eaglet? Was He friend or enemy? Was He part of the Vihangwanah? Was He come from our friends or was he unknown? And if He be the part of the Vihangwanah, so, why he did not tell us about Eaglet in that very moment at night?

- Suddenly, There came the sound of flapping wings and Mooni looked at up. Kite speedily coming down, with removing the branches of the Palsah tree. He landed near to Mooni.

"What is going on Mooni?" Kite asked in his stern voice, "How are you dear Eaglet? is everything right here?"

Eaglet only nodded after looking at him and Mooni said ahead, "It is looking good today's atmosphere, isn't it?"

"Yes, It is good from yesterday was, if we think about there some problem last night?" Kite questioned.

"Everything is right mate Woodpeck constructed this tree-hole so firm and strong that wind does not get inside then let alone the water of the rain."

Then, Kite made his voice extremely low and asked, "- and because of yesterday's stormy-rain lessened the chances of returning of the Father Eagle."

"Why, did my father not come back?" Abruptly Eaglet asked to Kite and Mooni.

"Perhaps, He might have missed his way because, of the rain, that reason, He would have gone to somewhere ealse. Therefore, he has been late." Mahina landed on the branch from air, and answered, she had gone to bring some fruits early in the morning.

Eaglet nodded on the answer but, Mahina casted a mysterious sight on Kite and Mooni.

In botom from the *Rose- Apple tree*, Safeda came out from his land hole. That whole was so, secured that rain water did not get inside, because, of intriculated roots of the tree, and also shape of the bark of the Rose - Apple tree.

"Gilhary!" Safeda called out.

Gilhary peeped out from his tree-hole on Rose apple tree and looking at down and said, "What happened Safeda?"

"Did you get information about our duty concerning about the coaching of Eaglet or timetable? Which task we have to finish or do?"

"No I have not got any information." Gilhary answered.

"Okay I am going out from the place for some time. If there, will be some message for me, tell when I shall come back." Safeda spoke.

"Message, will be given *us* first because, we shall have to convey it to other birds." Gilhary suggested with whiskling her tail, "I think president Lark, will take some decision today and also make timetable of our respective duty. Then responsibility will be placed on us."

"Now, I go. If today also will be rain here, I can not get a bit to eat. Good bye." saying this, Safeda jumped in other earth hole and disappeared with the last flicking movement of his white -thin-long-tail

This is the time of the evening. The Sun had left his last golden rays in the Brown and red sky. This is good atmosphere and there were no clouds of the rain around the Vihangwanah. Therefore, The daily work of Vihangwanah had been going on from the morning in better way. The water rush of the river had been deduced and the Fig tree which standing on the shore was still there and did not get any harm from the river water. But, Bagga had not come back on that elegant and the giant looking Fig tree.

After some time, fresh day light was chaged into coal like darkness and the silent spread over the great Vihangwanah. There was no one black cloud in the sky and stars had been overlooked in the blue sky. The silent of the Vihangwanah was being broken by the gushing sound of the river water and of the nocturnal animals. This is a sleeping time for everybird but everybody had not slept yet. The wooden swoop on the ancient *Babool tree*, which was front of the tree hole (as like door) was kept opened and Lark was pacing up and down inside (ancient) Babool-tree-hole that tree hole was very big and broad and there was great place inside it. The Moonight was coming brigntly in the hole from open swoop through the uncontrollable canopy of the thorny branches of the Babool tree. Lark seemed worried. There was diffrent types of colourful stones had been kept everywhere in his carved tree-hole, they were shining in various colours and that hole was fully glowing with the light (shining) of those. After some time Lark nodded his head nurvously, like he could not find out answer of the question. He went to one side of the hole which was decorated with different pictures and inscriptions and knocked with his beak on that special part.

Tuck s s s Tuck s s s Tuck s s s Tuck s s s Tuck s s s

- That sound was felt to be resounded at the every part of the Vihangwanah. As like that sound was a code of some type or it was code to call out somebody. That sound was mixed with the sound of gushing water and also breeze of air. There was no movement in the Vihangwanah for instance after that sound. But, some time after, the tree hole on the _tall elegant *Taramind tree*, which was far away from there, wooden swoop was opened and Raghu came out (The various coloured parrot) from the tree-hole of Taramind tree his various colour were shining like silken cloth (in The Moonlight). He did know that this was *sound code message* for him. He did not need to search that where the sound had come from. He realised that the sound code message was used for him before some time ago. He ever did not mind that to whom it came from. He did know that who used sound-message for him. He did not think for a moment. He just leaped away from the leavy branahes of the Taramind tree and spread his pracious wings. He was speedily covering the distance in The Moonlight. This was a late night time and no bird was accompnied with him. He was traveling over from the residence of woodpaek, Sugi and Robin .But, he knew that they will be in sound sleep at the moment. But, why was he called with the code message, it was unanswerable question for him. (He could not find the answer) But, He had not to wait for long time. He saw The Babol tree on some distance, where from that sound was, come some time ago. The tree of Babool seemed like a giant with the thorny branchas in The Moonlight. He easily turned him self. He saved himself from the thorny branches of the tree and landed near the opened wooden-swoop and with going two steps forward, he got into the hole.

"Did you call me, Lark?" Raghu asked in his robust voice. "What is problem?"

"I am sorry for bothering you so late night. But, there is something important." Lark said in apologise tone.

"Don't say sorry Lark, friend always helps friend and you are my best friend and It is my duty and-." Raghu said coming two steps ahead. "-It is not true that every bird sleeps at night time. Among them some think about tomorrow, don't they?"

Hearing this Lark spoke, "Yes It is true. I am also thinking about tomarrow and future and for that the Ineed your help."

Raghu nodded. As like he is suggesting that Lark ought to continue his talk ahead.

"-Everything happening strange here. I was elected as a president of the Assembly and also as adviser. But, I am not truely the president of the Assembly. Because, you have been elected for lots of time by birds of The Vihangwanah for presidentship. But, you never taken the post of the president. Raghu, this time also you had been selected for this post but you rejected that and I got the presidentship of the Vihangwanah. I really have to say that without you, I am totally incomplete in my thinking you know well. I always need for your help and "*In future also*," Lark humbly said.

"You are speaking all this clearly and it is the symbol of your meek heart. I will help you forever as my best friend and also the president of the asembly. " Raghu flapped his wings and said. His some feathers were disturbed by wind

"Thank you! Yesterday there was so heavy rain that I could not call you at my tree-hole and that reason I was unable to thinking about the education, waching and nurisng of Eaglet. I had thought once but, that was not right enough. I changed my thought for many times. Then I realised. That my thonght are inaccuarate without you and incomplete indeed so, I have to ask for your help."

Once again Raghu nodded his head and said, "What help you require from me. I am standing in front of you."

"First tell me how can we start coaching of Eaglet? Because, it is good time for his education and all types of the coaching. He is now engough old to learn all type of his education and if his parents had been here, his coaching would have been begun by now. This responsibility to us now and tell me how can everybird coach or teach Eaglet, with their help? You have got some idea on this point?"

Lark's eyes were glimmeing like pearl in The Moonlight and he was looking to Raghu for an answer, who was walking up and down. He stopped on one place and took a long breathe, and then He said, "I am thinking you, me and everybird and animals (Gilhary and Safeda) will be thinking on this matter at the moment. Yesterday I was thinking about this matter. We everyone have some distinction with us, we have something different quality in us. If we teach that unique quality to Eaglet. Then, he will be adept in his coaching and every skill."

Lark nodded once and looked at Raghu and asked, "but how?"

"Let me explain. Sona and Kite are great Fighter and hunters. Fighting is a part of their blood. If we assemble Sona and Kite. you will get the quality of Eagle and then we can easily teach him to hunting. Then Dove gives him knowledge of how to cure illness and Safeda tell him how to cure wounds. His present parents will give him the knowledge of what is importance of the life and teach him important chapter of life. How does catch fish from the water, Bagga will teach him about it and Bagga is one of the oldest bird of the Vihangwanah, That so, he can give him a lot of learnings. How does overtake danger on the earth and how does find out the way from there, this knowlege could be given him by Gilhary. Although Eaglet has no voice like Koel but, I think that she happily give him knowledge of how to inform any bird by the voice, when he will be in danger or how to convey his sad or happy thoughts from that tone to everybody. The Eagles make nest and this is inborne knowledg for them But, If Eaglet will not have seen any nest in his life then, It would be say that his knowledge will be deprieved but, Sugi can easliy give him the knowledge about weave the nest. Along with Sugi, Chidiya also give him that knowledge. After that, Robin can show him the experiment of how to fly through leavy branches, thorny bushes with adept quality and If he get late in night to come back home that time, how can find the right way from the position of stars and The Moon, this type of learing will be given him by Sona ."

Lark amazed after heard this all. He had not thought that Raghu could have made so perfect timetable for Eaglet's coaching. He said, " Raghu, you have made the great outline of the task, But, still you are forgetting some birds like I, you, Woodpeck, Parinda. and -"

"Kaka," Raghu completed sentence of Lark.

"Yes" Lark said, "Which responsibility will have to place on us?"

"Lark, you are the president of the respected Assembly, that resaon you think lot and make decisions. Therefore, you will not have any task or responsibility. I shall teach him how to use his beak as a tool because, we both have same type of beaks and I can tell him how to keen his beak with the help of wood. Woodpeack is skilled in everything. So, whatever work will be given for him, he would do that gladly and also he will teach Eaglet how to use the *sound code message* for help or for convey the messages. And now at last there is a still question about Kaka. I also did not think about Kaka. Which work we can give him for to do. I had no time to think about Kaka yesterday."

"We shall not have any benefit to think about him *(Kaka),*" Lark said disperately and quite angrily, "He hates Eaglet lot and along that he also hates me and other some birds. He contemplates *Safeda and Gilhary* very much. I have doubt that If we overhand some responsibility on him. He definitely will not do that. Perhaps, he will harm Eaglet. I am thinking that it will be better to keep him away from Eaglet and our coaching plan."

Raghu shook his head little and thoughtfully spoke, "your opinion is quite right Lark, and many birds do not like him. But, Kaka is an expirienced bird of the Vihangwanah. He has the great knowledge about every subject. He is aware about the direction and speed of The Moon and the Sun. He can easily understand the *foot-tracks or beak trails* of every bird (made by beak by any bird). Our ancestors, which knowlege or stories, had carved on tree trunks or other parts of trees, He can read that easily. He knows the differant types of birds lanaguags and also he adept in *foreign bird* languages. Some time I have to take his advice. He knows everything about everypart of our *legend*-history. So, I would think that If we ignore this type of knowledgeable and intelligent and adventurous bird. Then, that will be big blunder from us and he also great knowledge about nursing offsprings and therefore, we have to be him ready somehow for this work."

"Yes, He is an extraordinary bird indeed. But, I say you Raghu that for this task he definitely will say *"no"*. He will definitely reject our proposal." Lark, stopped for moment and asked, "But, why does Kaka hates Eaglet?"

Having heard the question Raghu laughted Lark amazed on the laugh of Raghu. But, did not ask any question. He was keep waiting till Raghu did not speak, "Listen! Kaka has many reasons to hate Eaglet. First Eaglet's colour is very white and Kaka's colour is dark black as a coal. That reason It is necessary for Kaka to hate that snow white coloured Eaglet. And then the Assembly of Vihangwanah has taken her decision against Kaka. Because, admitted that- Eaglet could stay or live at Vihangwanah forever .Therefore Kaka's anger was raised. After that, there is big reason for Kaka to hate Eaglet, that *Kaka's creed (Raven creed)* is the oldest creed in history and also in mythology of birds. Raven's creed has been allused in mythology and great advanturous stories of the birds. There are so many Epics which depicted the greatness of (black) Raven. But, now we are giving our full attention towards Eaglet because, the egle is our king and egle creed is more older than the creed of black Raven. We all respect to egle creed and that reason, abruptly, Kaka's higher prestige has been gained to dust. The egle is a convenance of the *God Vishnu*. That reason the egle is the oldest bird of the *"Vedas"* and *The Epics*. Therefore, Kaka is feeling affronted and dishounred. He had been used to for our respect but, now we are neglecting him because of Eaglet. Perhaps, He (Kaka) may using so disgust words for Eaglet.

"Yes it is right." Lark laughed and said. Then, he suddenly became sombre, "There is not any danger in the Vihangwanah but there is some mysterios situation in surronding and outsde of the Vihangwanah. That reason, Eaglet is living here with Mahina and Mooni should remain a secret and It is better If this should not be known to any other bird outside of Vihangwanah. This is our duty and our responsibility, we have to take this precaution that, Eaglet's security will not come in to danger."

"It is good point to think on," Raghu said, he was impressed, "We have to convey this message to every-friend of the Vihangwanah and also, There will be Two birds with Eaglet, when he will go to teaching or coaching (when he will be on coaching or training) Have you understood my point?"

Lark nodded positively Raghu was speaking ahead, "OK, then we have canvassed everything here and our timetable, whole timetable is ready now we shall think about Kaka sometime after. I call Sona, Robin and Safeda now. Therefore, we can easily work on the timetable." Having spoken this Raghu went inside one side of the tree hole and he knocked some part of the hole with his archead beak. Everytime various sound was come out from his knocking.-

Tuckss Tuckss Tuckss Tuckss

Tussckss Tussckss Tussckss Tussckss Tusscksss

Tuckck Tuckck Tuckck

That sound was resounded some time in the tree hole and also all over the Vihangwanah. At this night time that sound was supposed louder and supererior. After some time, sounds of flypping wings came in from out side of the tree hole of Lark. Then Sona, Robin and at last Safeda came inside the tree hole.

"Good night friends !" Raghu said.

"Very good night...... Good night." Sona said to Raghu and Lark respectively.

"Now you are thinking about why have you been called here so late in night and why did you make awaken from your sugar sleep also?" Raghu asked.

"There is no problem for me, Raghu - I sleep at day time and keep awaken through night. But, I must think that -" Sona saw towards Safeda and Robin -, "These two must have awaken from their deep sleep." Sona's eyes were glimmering and it was easy to find out where he was looking.

"If there is this type of matter so, we say sorry and apologize for bothering you. But it is really important meeting for us. From today Eaglet's coaching and training will be begun and about that we want to deliver some information to you. Safeda you and Robin too will convey this information to every friend of the Vihangwanah. Sona, you make yourself ready for coaching. Because, flying training will be given by you and Kite. so, inform about it to Kite also it is your task Sona. It is better both of you to make rest yourself for tonight and I have very important news to say you -," Raghu said with serious voice looking to Safeda, Robin and Sona one after another-, " that is Eaglet's residence of the Vihangwanah should be secret and no other should be informed about Eaglet execpt us. Now I give you timetable about Eaglet's coaching and who will give him which type of learning. I tell you that."

Then Lark and Raghu one by one gave all the information to Robin, Sona and Safeda and told them that, did not give any information to Kaka or Parinda (Because which work they will undertake that was not been determined yet.). Then Raghu asked, "Today morning I could not see Bagga on the Fig tree? Why?"

"Because, the day before yesterday he was weted by heavy rain, after then he came to my tree hole on that very night because, he thought that his Fig tree might have flown with heavy furious water of the river. Then he realised that very soon he must be sick so he went to Dove for treatment. I am sure that he will be taking treatment from Dove at the moment."

"If Bagga is not feeling well, then it is a bad news for us. I asked him about hundred times that he ought to be built a tree-hole for him but, he never listened to me. But, it is enough now. Robin listen me, convey my one message to Woodpeck, that He have to carv a big tree hole on any big and elegent tree. Because, for some time eaglet might be with Bagga in future and tell him also he have to make other tree hole on one another tree. Okay? "

"Fine? But Raghu, why do you want to make other tree- hole?" Robin asked.

Raghu casted sight on everyone and said, "sorry, friends! but I can't tell you about that and Robin,you tell to Woodpeck that second tree hole should be closer to first one but on different trees."

Robin nodded affirmative.

"It is okay then, best of luck to you all. From tomorrow a new chapter of our life will begin and there we have a responsibility to fulfill all our aims and goales. I hope that you have understood your responsibility and your role as well." Lark spoke. His eyes were glowing with hope.

"Definitely. All will be well and it is long night now and there is lot of work ahead us for tomorrow. so, give us bid now from this little meeting." Safeda humbly said to Raghu and Lark.

"Thank you. We expect better time in future. You may go now?" Raghu respectively said and bowed his head, his eyes twinkling in moonlight. Sona, Robin and Safeda one by one got out from Lark's tree-hole. For some time Raghu kept watching to them then he turned and went near to Lark.

"I take your leave; I have to make some preperation for tomorrow. If you have some need for my help. Just use *'sounding -code'* for calling me. I will come instantely."

Lark shook his head. Raghu made his way ahead and went out from the tree-hole. He streched his wings on air and leaped down. Lark came to the doorway of tree-hole to see him away. He saw, Raghu was flying on distance in darkness. Slowly he was flying on top.. He went away from the front of The Moon. That moment he was glimmered in moonlight. He was going away and away still, then, he transformed into black point and he was disappeared from eyesight of Lark.

****

THIRD

- By the next morning, Robin, Safeda and Gilhary had given timetable to everybird of their respective task and also who will keep watch on the tree-hole of Mahina and Mooni (on *Palsah tree*). - This timetable also had been made. Around, two khairrah trees from the Palsah tree, Woodpeck had been told to carve two tree-holes and for that work, he had been given time for some days. Therefore, watch-keeper birds could have watched over on the Palsah tree very keenly and protectively from Khairrah tree.

After that, on one morning Kite and Sona had reached to the Palsah tree, in front of Mahina and Mooni's tree-hole. There, Mahina, Mooni and Eaglet were waiting for them.

"-So, what are you going to teach Eaglet?"

"Mooni, flying is an important for everybird and it is the symbol of life. So - Eaglet should fly first and it is important. That reason, we shall help him to fly. We don't know, how shall we do that? And we don't know what the hazard in the flying is. Hence, we shall take away Eaglet to *the Tickwood forest* of near from here. There is season of shading leaves for the Tick trees and there will be grassy ground at the time therefore, if Eaglet falls down in the trying of his fly. He can not get hurt and He could easily survive then."

"Yes, Yes. It is good idea. But, If you are being with Eaglet so, what shall we do there?" Mahina qeustioned and looked to Mooni.

"Listen me Mahina, now you are guardians of Eaglet and therefore, which help you can provide to Eaglet that we both could not provide him. It will be motivation for him. It is his first attempt and you have to come with us. It will be helpful for us and it is important for his protection." Sona spoke positively and waved his head. Looking in eyes of Sona. Eaglet came closer to Mooni. He had not been habituated for Sona's voice or his yellow big eyes and also Sona could move his neck with full *360 degree.*

Mahina and Mooni become ready to go with Kite and Sona . Kite caught Eaglet in his solid -stilly claws delicately and before Sona, he leaped into air. Therefore, Sona could easily find them with his way. They all were making their way through branches, vines and numerous trees. They took two- three turns and arrived there where, they wanted to come. There were three or four tall tick trees in a row and no another bird was present there. Kite, Mahina-Mooni and Sona landed on one big bough of broad Tick tree, Kite made standing Eaglet on his legs near Mahina and Mooni. That was the tallest and most elegant tick tree over there. Air was flowing fast there because, that was the morning time and atmosphere was very clean.

"So eaglet, we have come here and from now onwards your practice, coaching and education will be begun from todays. We are present here for, we are going to teach you how to fly. so, are you ready to fly? " Kite softly explained. He was trying to being soft his voice.

"What? will you teach me how to fly?"

"Yes, we shall make you very perfect in flying believe us." Mahina said.

"My father was about to teach me flying before come here. He is a great hunter and great Fighter. He does fly very delicately." Eaglet informed them.

All four birds nodded their heads in consentment. They were seeming amazed.

"Now, look us how we fly. Then you will try to fly, won't you?" Kite spoke and stood on branch with preparation of fly. He spread his wings and controlled himself. Eaglet was observing this all with great concentration. Kite softly leaped away, he made his wings stable and moved downwards then he flapped his wings rapidly and flied on air. Now, he was flying stably then. He took two or three whirling on air and came back on the bough where, from four couple of eyes watching him. He asked to eaglet, "Did you look? How was I flying? Now be yourself ready and try to fly without fear."

"But, one thing we can do." Sona spoke to Kite, "when, Eaglet is trying to fly that time you hover down to this bough. So, If he failed to fly then you can catch him very easily therefore, he would not be got hurted."

Kite nodded his head in agreement and said, "Okay." Then he leaped down from the bough and after went down, He kept hovering.

Eaglet was ready to fly. He did not fear a bit Mahina, Mooni and Sona was taken aback by him. *(Probably his fearlessness)*. Because, they remembered their first experience of fly and at that time they were also standing on this type of bough with their parents. They were anxious as well as afraid with thinking of the first fly. But this eaglet was exception for that and he was not showing any fearness or any sight of frigntening. But Mahina, Mooni and Sona knew the reason why Eaglet did not fear. Because, that was Eaglet and there was nothing impossible for him. His flight was amazing and the Eagles can fly from thousand miles. That tradition had been infused in blood of Eaglet and that reason this hight was far less for him.

"Dear, when you will be ready, leaps down from the bough. Do not fear. If you are not able to fly, No problem yet, you not get hurt. Because, Kite is there and he will catch you."

He nodded his head on these encourageble words of Mahina. Once he looked towards sky and next moment leaped down from the bough. He tried to flap his wings on air but, he did not manage to fly. He was flastly going down and it is impossible for him to fly. He was feeling that all world is whirling with him. Suddenly he stopped in the air and he realised that he was caught by two steely clows. That were the claws of Kite and he took away him on the same branch of Tick tree where from he had leaped some time ago. There, Mahina and Mooni looking very worried. Because, Eaglet was seeming bewildered.

"No problem dear, at first time Nothing could understand Because, thie is new experience for everyone. Do not worry I am hoping that you must be successful in this second chance."

"I had never thought that, flying is so hard. I used to enjoying when I looked your flight. But now I realised, how much power you have to produce for your flight." Said this, the egle once again made ready himself to fly and Kite again kept hovering under that bough. Eaglet again jumped from the bough. But this time also he could not manage to fly. Kite had to catch him. After that, Eaglet tried to fly with new spirit, at this time he could manage to control himself for instance but, immediately Kite caught him in his powerful claws.

These all futile efforts of Eaglet was being watched by Kaka far from the distance tree and laughed scornfully as though, those unsuccessfull efforts of Eaglet were giving him lot of happiness. He muttered after saw those unssuccessful efforts, "These all birds are idiots totally idiots. This Sona was the greatest fool. This is day time and even though he came here. I don't know what can he see in this day light and other three birds are also idiots. They do not have a least idea about movements of eagle. I am strong feeling that they have never seen any flying eagle in their life time and if they will remain teach him to fly, like this. They themselves totally forget their fly very soon. They have committed a big blunder. On from which height, they are telling Eaglet to jump, actually that height is wrong, because, The air pressure is so high that. Eaglet could not fly. If they get him some down bough then he can fly easily because, eaglet get their flying strenght from their own blood. But who will tell this to these idiot birds. It was their mistake that they did not listen to me in assembly and they will never teach Eaglet anything without taking my help." After said contemptible words, Kaka casted his black sight on Eaglet and other four birds and flied away from there. Then he very instantly disappeared from eyesight and on which branch he had sited that again began to oscilate with forced-wind.

"I am really very bad in flying. I am really very ashamed that I could not learn how to fly today. You have taken my responsibility, although I was not your responsibility indeed!" Eaglet said with disappointment.

It was evening time and Eaglet was siting with Mahina and Mooni in their tree-hole on the *Palsah tree*. They had come back before some time when, Eaglet failed in his *Fifteenth* attempt and Kite only had been exericising himself, through catching him. But, after that, Kite and Sona, brought Eaglet on the Palsah tree and after saluting to Mahina and Mooni they held their way through their respective accomodations.

"You did attempt it very well. But, flying is not so easy to learn and after that you are an eagle and we don't know how make you fly? So, it is on you that you have to fly on your own strenght. So, for that fly you have to wait for some time more, perhaps." Mooni gave him consolation.

Having heard this Eaglet strenghtened and he became refresh. Eaglet went to doorway again and got out from there for some fresh air. Then Mahina and Mooni got privacy, it is from far days that they did not got privacy. They could easily hear two voices coming outside from the tree hole which belonged to Parinda and Woodpeck respectively. They both were keep watching on the Palsah tree.

"We should take help by Raghu or Kaka. Without that, we can not teach him, can we?" Mahina, sadly said to her husband- *Mooni.*

"Look Mahina, Raghu is very important bird and he is always having very important task with him. So, he can not always remain with us for guidence. We can not take his help. Now there is problem of Kaka, he is against us and Eaglet also that reason he does not come for our help. So, we do our attempt continuosly ourselves. Kite and Sona will definitely help him therefore, do not think about that. "

At the moment, flapping sound of wings came from outside the tree hole and along that Woodpeck and Parinda's greetings were heard also from the outside. Robin and Eaglet were entered within a moment (Mahina and Mooni glanced at each other questionably.)

"What is going on Mahina? How are you Mooni?"

"We are all right but, how do you manage to come here?"

"Oh! I have an important message that is Sona will come here for tonight and give Eaglet knowledge and learning about *stars and planets, position of planet* and *the zoadiac.*" Robin said

Hearing herd the name of Sona, Eaglet was terrrored but, he did not say anything.

"But, how it is possible Robin, he practiced lot today for flight and now study of the planets and stars will be far hard for him. He is very tired." Mahina said affectionately. As like, she had been a mother of Eaglet and Robin also knew how kind was she, that reason he spoke, "Do not take tension. Mahina. Woodpeck carved a big tree hole on a khairrah tree side by your this Palsah tree and Sona will give him this planetory knowledge on from that tree. This education will not take much time. Sona will give him only information about sky and stars."

"But is that so important because ..." Mahina spoke but, Robin did not listen his total speak and said, "Mahina you know that, what is more important and what is not and what would be better for him to get every type of education in the least course of time. That will help him for his whole life."

"Okay. If you are thinking it is right, then .... it will be right." Mooni said looking towards Mahina.

"But, I am afraid of yellow eyes of Sona also. He can move his heck very quickly and he is looking horrible. Instead of Sona, can Bagga not teach me all this learning or any other bird?" Eaglet worringly asked to them and they all also laughed on his qustion because, they knew that he, from long ago, had been afraid of Sona. Mahina went to his close and explained him, "Dear do not fear to Sona. Your and his creed is about to alike. Sona is the only one among us who can fly in darkness and also looks clearly. He is very kind with heart and after that, he has some knowledge about stars and sky and all directions. He can easily read the position of every planet and you will not need to go in his tree-hole. He will teach you planet watching and reading from by sided Khairrah tree. That teaching is an interesting part and you should not do hard work for that part. We all did not learn that well, but, you can learn it becasue of Sona. He will definitely teach you well and it will be useful?"

Eaglet nodded his head after hearing this all information and he made himself ready for all type of preparation.

"It is good ! Okay ! Then, I may ask for my bid now, I come again, If their will some message for you." Robin said, and he went out from the tree-hole, from which he had come inside some time ago.

Gloom had started to fall and stars now peeped out from blue sky. peace fully inhabited through the Vihangwanah. Watching duty had been changed and Gilhary and Safeda had come on to keep watch on the Palsah tree. At the very moment.-

Tusk sss Tucksss - kss - Tussss ck ssss -

This sound was resounded in the Vihangwanah. Raghu leaped on air from the Taramind tree and began to fly somewhere with his lezy wings. Wind was slow, although leaves of trees and shrubs were being shaken softly. He was sometime going out of sight because of his turning.As though he was playing Hide and Seek. Some time after, that greeny- tree area was sparsed and began the area of solid and rocky tablelands. There was huddle of bushes. Sound of the river's bouncing water was like the Fig tree where Bagga lived.

A big Mango tree was standing on some distance ahead and instantly Raghu got into intricable branches of the Mango tree and placed himself on a big branch of the tree. In front of the branch there was hole and wooden-swoop of the hole was kept open. Without any intimation Raghu straight entered into the hole, neglecting a small wooden plate, hanging by the door-way. Which bearing some ingraved / etched words-

"UNWELCOME GUESTS ARE MOST WELCOME HERE. "

Kaka was standing in front of him. This tree hole was an elegant one and moonlight made his way inside it very easily and greatly.

"How are you Raghu? How could you keep your legs in the tree- hole of mine?" Kaka asked and kept looking at Raghu with his harsh sight. "I heard your *sound code* message some time ago but, I did not believe on that you were coming in my tree-hole though, you have no need to deliver that signal for me. You could have come without an any indication."

Silently Raghu hearing all this. Then he said, "Look here Kaka. I have very important work and that can be done by only you."

"Raghu, I have never said "NO" for your work and will never say a "NO" for any work of you but condition is -" Kaka silently spoke, "- That work should be belonged to you...... only you."

Raghu thought on this point for some time.

"Listen to me Kaka! This work is not only importnat for me but, for the whole Vihangwanah. It is really important." Now, Kaka was thinking.

"I know that, you believe me Raghu, and I always be ready for your every little job or work. But, which birds do not give any respect to me or my decision either, for them I also do not take any responsibility. Although, the work will be in interest of the Vihangwanah. For your other jobs you have your other gentle friends, who will be ready to die on your one word." Kaka spoke. He was speakeing his every word with measure.

"Kaka, what will be the future of the Vihangwanah, which might be thought in future. But, look we should do all that which is in our hand. If anybody wants any help then, we should provide him that help whether, he is resident of Vihangwanah or outsider." Raghu spoke with coming two steps ahead and moolight fallen on him.

"Raghu, you are really brilliant and you can easily state your thought supperbly indeed. Now look you even did not take Eaglet's name and though, you prescribed all background of Eaglet - didn't you?" Kaka, said. Raghu could not understand that he was being eugolized or critisized by Kaka. Therefore, Raghu spoke, "You are great Kaka and thank for believing me. I am true *bird-friend* and I really don't want to hide.anything from you. You have to help us in Eaglet's training. Without your help we can't train him in every subject."

"A bird like me who is sticken to law, what could do for you? Likewise, you have many skilled and adept birds which can provide help to you and Eaglet also. That reason, I am needless bird. You all are very strong and useful."

"But, Kaka, there is some knowledge which only you can teach him but, no other bird even, I am not able to teach him that thing. (That thing only you can teach him.) we have many skilled birds, Although, *Law knowledge* could be given by only you, there is your need all of us. You are the only bird who can tell him about the real laws of the Vihangwanah and you are very skilled bird in every type of bird language. You can easily recognise every dialect of every bird. You are expert in *"stars and planetory reading."* Therefore, you can give Eaglet better education than any other bird of the Vihangwanah can." Raghu said in counseling tone.

"Aohoho----- Raghu, But, which last night the Assembly meeting had been held, in that meeting you called *Sona* as an intelligent bird and in the law, Sona was called as even more intelligent bird than me. so, How can you now calling out me as the most intelligent bird in the Vihangwanah? And how in *The Law Provence* specially?"

"OH! Your memory is extremely amazing Kaka. It will be lessen If, I in my words praise you upto the moring from tonight. *That* Assembly night, I was in anger that reason I spoke very furiously at the Assembly, but, that was not totally wrong one. Look, Kaka ! Sona, is older than (other birds of the Vihangwanah). He is evidence of which hard work his ancestors had done in making the rules of the forest and it is right that he has a great knowledge of the laws and If my words would have hurt your feelings. Then, *I say sorry* for my mistake and for my words. But Sona is knowledgeable bird and he is useful and it is right time to use his all knowledge for Eaglet." Raghu humbly spoke.

"Don't say sorry Raghu untill, there is a matter about every knowledge and law, I know that you are the greatest bird in the Vihangwanah and you are superior than me." Kaka respectly said, "sometime I also ask you for some problem. You have very great skills and adept mastery in every subject. Many times you have solved some problem of mine. You are one of the powerful bird of the Vihangwanah. so, why do you not give this all education to Eaglet yourself. If you have such a great quality after that, why did you come to me?" Kaka asked. His voice was very calm.

Raghu hesitatingly shook his head and spoke ahead, "Kaka, I do not have every answer at the moment of your question and If I have an answer it is not possible to tell. Please believe me only you -who have to give coaching to Eaglet. When there will need for my guidence that time I shall give that education or learnings. But, at this time everything depends *on you* and there is need for your help at the moment."

"I shall not do any help upto there is the matter about that eaglet. sorry I can't do any help to anyone. There is no relationship between Eaglet and me. I do not have any contact with his coaching also. I have been against him and even now my decsion is not changed. I am ready to do help other birds If there will need but, I can not help Eaglet indeed." Kaka spoke in one breathe and this time his every word drizzeled with spite.

"I would have thought through every view. If, I were in your place. I would have thought about walefare of the Vihangwanah first. You know Kaka, how Eaglet is important for us and what depend on him of the Vihangwanah so, only for that reason we should be left our all rivelry and jalously and work unitedly. You should help these birds, who are trying to teach that eaglet." Raghu said with emotion.

"Who even does't know on from which hight, Eaglet should be given flying training, what I shall do collaborate with them? They even should have known even about this fact." Kaka spoke evily.

On this description of Kaka, Raghu lightly smiled and said, "*Yeh....yeh....* It is right that those birds have no great knowledge about it but, Kaka after some days. your past will be again standing in front of your eyes and If I had knowledge of these all things, and anybody had been doing any mistake in front of my eyes that time, *I would not have sited on a branch of the tree comfortably and would not have laughed and taunted on them* but, I had joint them and helped them in their work instead."

Having heard this, Kaka bounced with fear and looking amazed, "But, Raghu- How could you -"

Hearing no complete speech from Kaka Raghu forworded, "Which Mango tree is your residence, has been long and ancient history behind it. The mango trees have been great place in *"epics"* and *"vedas"* and *"all myths-legends"* and I know your deep ancient study . There is great importance for mango tree either there is beginnings of new life, festivals or any celebration. This tree is symbol of victory and success. You know it well and you have made *"The King of fruits"* as your Home (tree-hole) but hereby, I announce one thing which is important that, your nurture is far older and more greater than this mango tree. That tradition is very deep one and that is part of your blood. You should have great respect of your tradition and nursing and I wish that you see your glorious *race past* and then help us. If you want because, your blood is pure blood from that tradition which was very helpful to us and can be.... in future also. So, untill that time, Good Night."

Raghu once looked at Kaka and nodded his head. Then he came out from the tree hole and leapad on air. Kaka heard low flapping sound of his wings. Kaka still not moved from his place like that he was thinking on that suprising qustion which Raghu had laid in front of him.

Sona and Eaglet had sited on the branch of a Temp-tree (out from the tree hole.) The night was very fresh and there was not scent of rain which fallen down two nights before. On the place of clouds, stars rainning on from all sides in blue sky and low breeze of night was feeling quite pleasing. After having taken pleasure from that beautiful night, Sona spoke, "Dear eaglet, now we take information about stars and planets so, on from you can easily find out way of your tree hole and easily go to there in night time."

Eaglet saw Sona, his eyes now seeming very penetrative even then, Eaglet sited by his side (They were very near on tree branch, which was by the side of the Palsah tree, where Mahina and Mooni lived.)

"But, these stars and planetory is looking far away from here so, even then how could we get our perfect way or path by planetory?"

"Yes, yes very right, it is impossible to reach on that height. But, If we do study from this planetory then we can get right judgement of time. Every planet moving with different direction and their speed is also changeble and every planet has his independence and special exitance above in the sky." Sona explained to Eaglet. "Don't fear, this time you only will be informed about name of every star and planet because, you are not still enough mature to memorize all speciality of every planet. So, only look at me and mind on my information and name of the stars which will be given to you. Look here and hear me carefully."

Eaglet nodded (once) and looked to Sona with enthusiasmly. He did not know exactly Sona was so intelligent and he never looked to Sona with so, curiously. He sunddenly thinking that, He was very used to Sona and he known Sona very well from long long time. Now Sona began to talk, looking towards the blue, full with stars sky, "Look, that *purple* is the planet satern and it is only planet that is having around it a circle and its colour is *Brown*. Afterthen that is *Mercury* which is glimmering in white colour and it is near to the Earth."

"Then there is *Mars* that is having *Red colour* and *The Jupiter* who is the biggest planet in the universe and that glimmers like *Redish and Brown*. And then there is *Venus- it rises in the night for six month and then again after six month It rises in dawn time*. His colour is faint brown. Some time he rises form the east and some time from the west and there last but most and not in least that in very high in the sky and very rediant is *"the pollar star"* means *"Dhroove"* star. It never moves from its space and that, you can see globe of *silver colour, It is The Moon* and it is an important planet but, it is not really planet or star but it is the natural setellite of our beautiful earth. Now did you understand what I have told you about our planetory?"

"*A ...... little bit* ......can you show enough kindness to tell me again these all information?"

Sona laughed open heartly on the question of Eaglet but, after then he told once again Eaglet all information with silent tone and this time Eaglet looked more satisfied than erliar.

"- Okay Dear eaglet. It is long night and you might have tired now and it is better to go our tree holes." Sona said at last.

"But I have an important question."

"Good ! question is always symbol of success and asked freely ! What you will be in your mind? " Sona amazingly said.

"This is The Moon long in the sky. But I can see some dark dots on his surface. So, tell me what is that dots mean? The Moon is looking very bright .Neverthless, how he became the owner of these dots?" Eaglet aksed, He continuosly staring to The Moon, and was seeming like any *silver globe* because of his white colour.

"You asked very good question but, for the answer, I have to tell a long story and we would have to be some time for that and at the time we don't have enaugh time. So, I will give answer of this question in tomorrow's class. Now, let's hold our way of tree-holes." Sona said and caught Eaglet in his warmy claws and after once high leap, he flied through that silver night beams. When Sona reached on very distance place with holding Eaglet. He did't have any idea that some bird was looking them (from) long time on from one high sprig of an elegant *Mullbury tree*.

****

FOURTH

"- So, now it is clear that he will not help us by any way?" Raghu spoke.

"-You are just talking like that he used to help us lot in the past." Lark said smilingly, "I have told you about thousand times, Havn't I? That Kaka could not be explained by any one and now I think you probably understood what I meant to say."

Raghu came straight to Lark, after his last and *black* meeting with Kaka in last night. He told everything to Lark. Raghu spoke ahead, "Yes. It is absolutaly right. I tried with my heart but, unfortunately I failed. How Kaka is large with his knowledge, more than he is much smaller with his heart. Now, we should give full help to ourselves. Without our help Eaglet can't get better education."

"Okay. I had asked Woodpeck to carved a tree -hole on a khairah tree for Bagga? How that work is going on?" Raghu asked.

"That tree-hole is ready and it is very strong and looking good. Woodpeck made two Tree-holes as you gave him instructions and these are situated on a *Mohagani tree* by the Palsah tree, where Mahina and Mooni live. But, there is still bad news." Lark informed.

"Which?"

"Bagga refused to stay in the Tree- hole, though Tree-hole's having been ready. He went on that Fig tree which standing by the shore of the river and where he has been living from long time. I got this information by Robin." Lark sadly said.

"Bagga will never listen to anyone. How many times I told him don't live on open branch. It would be danger for him. This time is very bad and every bird has responsibility on his shoulder. (About Eaglet). Has Robin not told him which responsibility we have put on his shoulder at the moment?"

"Yes- Yes .... Bagga came back on his Fig tree today from Dove. (Bagga had been ailed because of heavy rain, and he was staying with Dove because, Dove was a great philosopher of medicine.) And he has been informed about his mission also. But there is still time for that mission Raghu. Because- ,"Lark desperately said, "- Eaglet can not fly least one feet yet and without a knowledge of flying we can not teach him other subjects. Only Sona is giving him education about Planetory *and star reading* at night. Only that thing he can learn now. We have to wait for some time more. "

Raghu only nodded his head and looked at Lark who was standing from back to him and was looking out The Moonlight from the tree-hole entrance.

Moving of The Earth and the Sun and time just was vapourising like air and going ahead. Days of the Vihangwanah had never passed so rapidly. But, from when, Eaglet had been to the Vihangwanah, from that moment our birds did not know about how many days were surpassed. By the days Eaglet's coaching continued only concerned about *flying and planetory reading*. Because, untill Eaglet does not get good knowledge about how to fly. It was in vain to give him any other coaching.

That was Rainy days therefore, between these two days there was heavy rain and that reason, Eaglet was become free from every type of coaching. Till now, *Parinda, Bagga, Sugi, Dove, Safeda, Gilhary, Koel, Woodpeck,* and *Robin* did not have their turn of coaching on them. Because, Eaglet's progress was not with the day's measure. This was really bad news for every bird.

"I think, perhaps We are doing a big blunder in coaching of Eaglet, otherwise no bird does get so much time to take a fly." One day Sona said to Kite while they were standing on a *Sycamore* tree with relaxed state.

"Look. We -anybody from us, do not have any notion about how to train Eaglet except Kaka one. But he totally refused for proposal and if he had said *"yes,"* Then, I don't think anybody would have been happy to hearing him. Becasue, he knowingly would have mistaken in our work. Wouldn't he?" Kite said

Sona nodded and said, "I am waiting for that day when Eaglet will fly independently!"

For this event birds of the Vihangwanah did not wait for long time. But, which incident happened on that very day, was very unbelievable indeed. That day was holiday for everybody (which, used to come once in every month, except those birds who were on watching duty on Mahina and Mooni's Palash tree. Because, watcher birds always having duty.) It was an evening time, Eaglet was passing - time in his tree-hole with Mahina and Mooni *(It was holiday for him also.)* and he was little sad because he did not get out from his hole for whole day. Wind was becoming lezy and The Sun was getting retirement from his respected work, there Koel and Dove were having watching duty on Mahina and Mooni's tree.

Mahina and Mooni heard some flapping sound out of their tree-hole and without moment and without calling, Kaka got into the tree hole. He was walking impressively. *It was his first time to came into their tree hole*. Comparing to his tree hole, It was too small and not enough artistic.

"Kaka, you are here?" Mooni bounced. With amazement and said, "welcome......! Kaka .... welcome."

"I am not feeling happy after heard your greetings Mooni or don't think that I am happy to came in your tree-hole. I have an important task and that reason, I am here at the moment." Kaka talked in low rude voice, "I came here to take away Eaglet with me for teach him how to fly."

Hearing this account Mahina and Mooni got amazed and Eaglet gazed towards Kaka.

"But, Kite and Sona have taken all responsibility of Eaglet and they will teach him-"

"It is wrong supposition that, If anybody take any responsibility so, after that it could be completed by him and likewise, it is visible that which coaching has been given by them to Eaglet. How excellent that is !" Kaka didn't hear even a word from Mooni or Mahina and turned to Eaglet, "He can't fly atleast one feet hardly. How greatly have been taken all his responsibility by Sona and Kite, you can see that, Can't you?" Kaka smiled scornfully.

"Yes, but they are trying...." Mahina spoke ahead.

"Believe me. I don't have trivilous time to talk with you here. Will you send Eaglet with me or not? Because, I have other works to be completed and I don't have time for this strange eaglet. But there are some reasons, for that I have come here. I can train him in fly. If, you permit me for his coaching...."

Now, Mahina had become angree on Kaka's speaking. Mooni put his wing on her back. Before she is giving any unhonourable answer to Kaka, Mooni said, "Okay, You can take away Eaglet with you. But, who is coming with you?"

"No one," Kaka talked in peaceful voice, "-and don't send anyone. Only me and Eaglet. I don't want other bird with me. I will see what happen."

At the moment, there spread pin dropped silent. With breaking that silent, Mooni went on to Eaglet, "Dear! Go, with Kaka, he will definitely give you good experience about fly." On these words Mahina only looked to Eaglet and he also nodded his head positively.

"Okay then, I will catch up you from outer branch of the tree. " Kaka directed to Eaglet and went out from there without talking a word to Mahina and Mooni. Eaglet walked back to Kaka. That time Mahina or Mooni were still standing there and looking at the leaving eaglet. After coming out from doorway Kaka leaped up on air and then he held Eaglet in his two claws softly. After then he flapped his wings rapidly and then he obscured above *safron colourd* sky with Eaglet.

Mooni got out with Mahina from his tree hole. He said, "Don't worry Mahina. I send Kite after them (Kaka and eaglet)." He leaped on air and disappeared in green shadding trees, also got beyond from Mahina's eyesight. Koel and Dove were seeming perplexed, after espied this all. They were on duty of watcher on the Palsah tree of Mahina and Mooni.

Kaka was flying fastly above from greeny land. He was flying from long time therefore, It was boaring journey for eaglet. He asked, "Kaka! How will still we have to fly yet?"

But, he wasted his breath only. Because, Kaka did not open his beak by inch for the answer. After some time greeny land changed into rocky one and then Kaka landed on a mullbury tree and he took placed Eaglet on same branch. It surrounded by some top trees and grounds.

"You might have observed many flying of birds therefore, you know how to fly and once experienced how to fly as well. Now, I am taking up you with me high in the sky and then drop you down from there-"

"What?" Eaglet shouted fearly. But, Kaka still talking ahead, like there was not obstacled between his talking, "-Then you would have to fly, If you don't fly. I don't do anything for you. After that, you will definitely bang on this rocky ground and I don't know what will happen with you after that?"

"But-" again, Eaglet tried to open his beak, It was gone in vain, "I hope, that you get all. What I said you. Now be ready. I am taking you with me high in the sky."

Now Eaglet was thinking about either he came there for to learn fly or getting his bone ramshackled. But, In any case, now time had gone very far from his hands *(or claws) and* Kaka was taking him away upwards. After gone high in the sky. He was dropped by Kaka from his claws. It was just shock for him, he could't believe that Kaka could do this type of act. He was whirling in air and rapidly falling downwords. Kaka only slowly flying onwards and gazing at Eaglet, who was going more fastly downwords.

"*Kaka*! What have you done this?" Kite speedly leaped on Kaka. He was smoothly flying.

"I did't do anything and but how do you come here?" Kaka easily asked question. Eaglet still rapidly going down and he was very near from the rocky ground.

"I shall give an answer of your question after some time, I want to save Eaglet first, otherwise he will dash on rocks and ...."

Suddenly, Kaka came front of Kite and spread his wings with saying, "Do not go to him. At the moment he belongs to me and further, He will not teach flying if, you go there."

"He does not belong to *you.* At the moment, I think. He belongs to *death.* If I do not go there, then-" Kite tried to thrash away Kaka by one side. But, when he saw down, that time he witnessed that Eaglet flapped his wings at *Ten -Fifteen feet up* from the Earth and he was hovering there with his tiny white wings.

Kaka gazed to Kite for some time and he went down without said a word to Kite. Eaglet could not manage to fly himself on air far long time. He landed himself on thorny bush. Kaka pearched by his side.

"Kaka! I can fly. I learned how to fly- did you not look, Did you?" Eaglet shouted in joy and flapped his tiny wings. Kaka not bothers to his beak any more. He flied in air at the same time Kite approached to him, "I know you have been sent here by Mooni but, I would be happy, If Mooni had believed me. I hope you will carry away Eaglet to Mahina and Mooni. And convey my one message to him say him to make a favour on me, if he do not tell that I trained Eaglet in flying and you also don't tell anyone this and say everybody that you have taught flying to Eaglet. It is my request to you." Kaka said after that, without saying a word to that happy eaglet or looked to him or did not mind on Kite, who was trying to say something, Kaka speedly disappeared into distant ambiguous and tall and green tops of giant trees.

Kite was very happy because of Eaglet could fly little bit and learnt it well. when, little time after, they left that place, time Eaglet flied with Kite till some distance and this was first time Eaglet, was not feeling two steely claws on that help he used to fly and look down to running Vihangwanah. This was very happy moment for him. This was first happy moment for him when from, *his father left him in the unknown Vihangwanah.*

As like conflagration this happy news spread all over the Vihangwanah and happiness was got new spirit like gush. Everybird was greetings each others and meeting with complemently and over joyidly .No one informed about Eaglet had been taught his flying by Kaka. This all was like any *festival* for Vihangwanah. Which had been not celebreted from long time. But, Kaka did not become the part of all this celebration, even he was not seen by anyone after his training session with Eaglet. On the next day there a party was orgnised in this escatic mood, which was to be celebrated by the River shore, under *The Big Banyan tree.* This announcement was declared by Lark and that was to be held on the following eve. All these messages were conveyed to everyone by Robin, Gilhary and Safeda. But, Robin gave Lark the information about Kaka that he was not in his tree-hole on the Mango tree and no one had seen Kaka anywhere. Except Kaka, every bird and two animals accepted the invitation happily for the great banquet.

"This type of celebration is being held here after many years. Even, I forgot that how benquet is. But, it is great and very proudable moment for all of us." Safeda was telling to Gilhary.

"Oh - yeh------- I was small, that time one banquet had been held here. Because, Sona had won a big Fight over a big Owl, Who was looking to conquer the Vihangwanah *(that time Sona was president of the Assembly)* But, Sona had very bravely beaten him and broke his dream to become *Monarch* of the Vihangwanah." Gilhary made Safeda imformaed.

On the other hand, another of distance tree on high branch Koel and Chidiya were speaking to each other. It was night time. But, everybird was still awake, because, It was special day for every-Vihangwanah-resident. It did not happen before ever.

"Eaglet got knowledge and information about fly and he can fly now. How good it is! Our bird- friends are able to tought him all this. It is very respected and glorious win for us. Now, I believed that from now onwards he will learn brilliantly."

"OH...... yes and tomorrow there is banquet for everyone. It is not wonder, it was to happen one day. After some years, when Eaglet got his all education and become complete in his skill and education that time he will be the king of Vihangwanah and it will really suit for our forest." Koel said in her sweet honeyied voice.

"Yes, it is right and It will definitely happen one day." Chidiya said with a breathe, "- But Koel, Untill It is our duty to protect him from every harm and danger situation."

Moonlight was falling on Koel and Chidiya and on which branch, they had been resting, that was moving with cold breeze of wind. But Koel or Chidiya did not disturb by any movement of trees, from their talk. They were looking like, perhaps, they will spend away the whole night in this happy atmosphere.

Next day was not lessen than *"Diwali"*. Every bird made some decoration on their trees and in their tree hole also but, except Kaka. Today no bird did have to attend on any duty. This was a great holiday for every one. One of the biggest holidays this ancient Vihangwanah had ever seen. In very morning Eaglet had flied with Mooni on Berry *bushes* which were near from the Palsah tree. This was his first independent fly on those bushes. He tasted the most delicious and juicy berries of red and green colours. Then he again returned with Mooni to his tree-hole. Till now, many birds had been coming to Mahina and Mooni's tree-hole and they had given wishes to Eaglet and Mahina and Mooni also. Because, they had done very great work for made Eaglet fly. Koel, Kite, Safeda, Sugi all had visited at morning time, while at afternoon time, Parinda, Woodpeck, Bagga, Dove, Gilhary met them. Everyone of them got some fruits, different types of flower's and Honeycomb as gifts for him. (Some fruits were so rare that, Eaglet had not seen any other fruit like that.) But, there was great moment when, Safeda shown his gift and It was just beautiful *and* the rarest *and* prestigious *and* the richest one.

He had brought an Amulet which was made by leather but at the center of that amulet, there was a prestigious triangular shaped small stone of Red colour and it was shining like blaze of the bonefire and a petal of a wild- flowers. Safeda delivering his thought when, he was giving it, "The leather that belongs to the amulet is very ancient and it came form *"The Harboury"* animal and the Red stone, you are looking, it is very prestigious and priceless one. It shines in darkness (*when, It is got Moon light*) and It is supposed, that it protects you from every harm and be your luck strong." When Safeda stopped his talk, Mahina asked him, "- then why did you not wear some amulat of like this?"

"Oh.... It was very precious stone and to be not found very generally. It is very rare and I wonder, I had got this one some time ago. But, how could I get this stone I don't know indeed. I am sure, It is only two or tree in the Vihangwanah and. it is second one because, some years ago, I found one and recently I also got this one. I had to give something special to Eaglet that reason, I thought, it was the only thing which I could give to Eaglet." Safeda enthusiastically storied.

"Thank you Safeda,"Mooni said, "- Then, today's evening, in banquet. This precious amulet will be locked around to your neck. Okay!, Dear eaglet?"

Eaglet nodded his head happily and glared at the glimmering Red stone which was fixed in centre of the Amulet.

It was evening time and it was most happiest evening at the Vihangwanah (undoubtedly) yet, The Sun was to be set and his red - brown coloured globe was ambiguosly visible on back of the mountains, (The Sun was peeping out behind from rocky mountains) Clean blue sky and roaring wind was giving a prelude of happy mood. Now some flying birds had been in the sky.

Eaglet was going to banquet place with Mahina and Mooni. He was very excited for his first dark-evening fly and also, it was first time when he was to fly so long.

When they three (Mahina, Mooni and Eaglet) were reached to the banquet, they had little late because, In the term of Eaglet's flying, He had taken *five* important stops on various trees.

"It is really troublesome." Eaglet said at last, "It wants great power and you have to waste also lot of power." When he flied in the shade of the *Big Banyan tree* with Mahina and Mooni, that time every bird flapping their wings as like, they were welcoming them and specialy to Eaglet. In that Sona, Bagga, Raghu and Kite flapped their wings very speedly and loudly. While, Gilhary and Safeda jumped on air for some time. Then again Mahina, Mooni and Eaglet was rained of wishes and greetings by Raghu, Sona, Lark, Robin (who were not able to come at Mahina and Mooni's tree-hole, because of their busy shedule.)

Gilhary and Safeda made a cricle by rocks and stones. In that cricle, They had set a bonefire and around that bonefire, there was placed many types of delicious fruits and Bagga was stedily gazing them with his eager eyes.

"May I have your attention please, Thank you!" Lark Addressed laudly because, everybody was busy in chating with each other, "everyone knows, for what reason this banquet organized here. Our little hero now learnt how to fly. He learnt fly and it is great news for us. Good! Very good! We have already congratulated him for his great success. But now we shall congratulate those birds who have taken great hard work for this coaching. They are Sona, Kite, Mahina and Mooni .So we are going to flapp our wings for them." on this point every bird flapped their wings for them.

"Thank you! Thank you! Very much." Mahina, Mooni, Sona and Kite said looking to everyone.

"I am Lark, the president and adviser of the Vihangwanah Assembly, welcome you all here on this great banquet .Only Kaka is not present for this banquet. Becasue, He was not at Vihangwanah today. he might have gone to somewhere for his work. May be out of the forest. Now, It is the time to give the present to Eaglet which was brought by sefeda for him" Lark said and he touched his beak on earth by his side and lift up the amulet. The central peace of the amulet was glimmering in bonefire's light. It was shining like glorious planet. Eaglet was taken aback to see the amulet there and he whispered in Mooni's ear, "But, this amulet was in our tree-hole and now it is here? How it reached here?"

"What are you thinking, there is not any mystery which is hidden in the Vihangwanah?" Safeda, who was standing back to Mooni, he heard Eaglet's question and he was answering now, "- and don't think those all mysteries you can understand in some days."

Mahina and Mooni also nodded their head on this description by Safeda.

"Now, I request Mahina and Mooni to tie up this amulet around neck of Eaglet." Lark humbly requested going two steps ahead, and he handed over. The precious amulet to Mahina and Mooni. Eyes of everybody were sticked on that *Red stone* of the amulet and It was sparkling in the blaze. Mahina and Mooni tied it around the neck of Eaglet, helping with each other. Now he was seeming like a prince.

"It is looking nice dear, be your luck strong with blessings of the amulet." Kite energetically said. (Eaglet was his student) when, everyone praised the amulet then Lark said went on, "Thank you everyone. So, now it is time to begin a party and I request to everyone go and freely taste every kind of fruits without any hesitation. Again thank you."

At the very moment, birds began chated with each other in group and every fruit was being tasted by them. Sona, Safeda, Mahina, Mooni and Eaglet were talking with each other in group. After taking big bite from a Jamoon fruit, Safeda asked, "Sona, I had given you a prestigious stone of Blue colour, like this one. Have you kept that one protected or not?" His eyes were fixed on eaglet's Amulate.

Hearing birds had to wait for Sona's answer, beacuse he had in his beak a big bit of wild Berry, when he gulp it, he said, "Yeh...... Yeh...... I did not forget that day when you had given me that stone and it was happened because of Two accidents and I also remember that great Fight and pounce which befallen on me."

"Which *pounce*? Which *Fight*?" Eaglet asked. He was not still eaten a bite, because, he had taken a Wallnut to eat and he was hammering on it with his beak therefore, It was seeming dangerous because of hammering his beak was reached on the breaking edge. It was visible that the Wallnut was to be broken his beak very soon.

"Dear eaglet, that was combat for me. The first battle of my life," Sona was speaking with more enthusiasm, "Mahina and Mooni would know all-" Sona asked. On that, Mahina and Mooni, who both are busy in eating an Apple berry, nodded their head affirmative. "Believe me, Dear eaglet, that time. I was recently learnt how to fly and my family was in felicity. After that, some days were carried out in happy state. Then, I alone used to go on flying far from my tree-hole and it happened on same day morning, did't it Safeda? Safeda was small that time and on that morning he also had got to out for some work. Same time Safeda was attacked by a huge Falcon. But I was in air, and I watched it all I ran for his help. I fought with the Falcon for some time. He was more bigger and more stronger than me, But at last he accepted his defeat, he couldn't win and he ran away from there. Right Safeda?" Safeda nodded his head on Sona's description and said, "I tell you eaglet. If Sona was not there for my help, I would not have alive and after this incident we became best friends of each other. But, after then, there happened again some thing more deathly and dangerous-"

"-more dangerous and deathly but what?" Eaglet asked. At last, he cracked the Wallnut and started eating raisins from it.

"That time, All Vihangwanah was present there, it will be not a hyperbolic statement, if I said it and that was one of the ghastly and dangerous Fight of the Vihangwanah." Mahina said biting a bit from black Grapes. Her voice was shivering.

"That all still in front of my eyes." Mooni stated. He was also lost in the past.

"But clearly what actually happened?" Eaglet asked with eagerness.

"That was evening time and Safeda had come out from his Earth hole. He was on searchings of his food. Then suddenly a *Big White Owl* came to attacked on him and he caught Safeda in his powerfull claws. Safeda and owl were of same colour. It was just part of my and also Safeda's luck that I was around there on that time also. I attacked on the white owl. Safeda was dropped by his claws and securely landed on grassy land. We both were engaged in our battle very soon. After a little time every bird of the Vihangwanah gathered there, only Raghu was not present there. I said everyone to stay far away from our Fight because, I did not want anyone get hurt from them becasue of our Fight. We both were the best and both were skilled in our movement, so that reason, It was difficult to beat each other. The white owl had come from abroad and his skills were different. But, I was the resident of *The Vihangwanah* and this forest was my master for very long time. We were fighting, when The Sun set and evening came, that time the white owl became exhausted and I did not miss that opportunity. Then I so furiously dashed him that he got injured and collapsed on a bush and I stood on his bosom. Then everyone flapped their wings for me as my praise and my win over the white owl. After then white owl beg forgivence from Safeda and he vowed that he would never come to Vihangwanah again and I remembred. On very next day, there was great banquet had been held for my great victory. That was announced by Kaka because, that time Kaka was the advisor and the president of the Assembly. After that banquet there was never held such a banquet again. But, I should accept that, *this banquet is more greater and precious than that one.*" Sona became emotional and spoke ahead, "- when I first time rescued Safeda that time I got priceless reward of his *friendship* and then again I rescued him from the white owl .That time he gave me a precious stone of *Blue* colour and tht is the only one. But, I like first reward more than second one. That is friendship of Safeda, always friendship is greatest treasure and there is not other reward as prestigious as friendship is. *Friendship always helps you, If you preserve it.*"

After having heard these statements from Sona, everyone, who listening him, nodded their heads affirmative to show that, they all were agreed with Sona's thoughts.

Time was going ahead and ahead and banquet was also progressing with the time. Everyone was chating and eating something (*There was river water for drink*). Till now, Bagga had eaten one Pomegranate, an half Watermelon, Three Apple -Berries and four Sunflowers. ("-you ought to concentrate on the work, which you are doing." - He said.)

Mooni was standing alone in one side. Mahina talking with another bird, while Eaglet was standing with Dove and Koel. Raghu went to Mooni and said, "Kaka, did not come today."

Mooni looked at Raghu and nodded his head, but he did not say a word, looking that Raghu spoke, "I am thinking that, It will be better, If you do not tell anybody about Kaka!"

Having heard this from Raghu Kaka was taken aback, "How do you know that I was thinking about Kaka?"

"Mooni, perhaps you are forgetting that, you are talking with that bird, who has refused the presidentship of the Assembly himself about Four times. (So, how fool that bird will be?)" Raghu gently said and laughed, "Do not tell to anybody that Eaglet has been trained into flying by Kaka. He requested you and it will be the dishonour of his request, you all birds have been taking great hard-work behind Eaglet's education. You, Kite, Sona and Mahina, you had learnt him his very first flying. That reason, it is your triumph so, all honour goes to you four birds and you and Kite are only birds who know, Kaka taught him how to fly and If there is something problem. Then, I already told Kite an excellent- reason for the satisfaction of all birds. He will tell that reason to them, if there will happen something opposite. Okay then? and Mahina I know her well, she is your wife and she always stands behind you strongly. (She will not tell anybody a truth.)So, it is not about in her bussiness. She is happy because, Eaglet (is) the part of your family now and it is great moment for every bird when he *fly* at first time and second one will be when he *hunt* for himself- But, There is still time for that. This is the starting of eaglet's life. we have to wait his maturity and time has an answer of everything. so keep this subject by side at moment. Everything is right now. Okay!"

Raghu placed his one wing on Mooni's back, "Raghu, untill you are with me, No trouble can overtake me. You are transcending the imagination and understanding. Tell me how did you know for what about was I thinking?" Mooni asked again.

"You are thinking about Kaka when you were asking this question, then -" Raghu said with laugh and walked away from there, "- How can I answer you?"

With the company of Moon, bonefire's light was feeling better and in this atmosphere Lark attracted everybirds attention and announced -, "Please, may I have your attention. Please, do not stop your eating and enjoying. Thank you. We have to be more conscious and alert and how did we manage to hide an identity of Eaglet, like that, we shall have to hide it in future also from strangers, got it?"

Everybird and Two animals (Gilhary and Safeda) nodded their heads on Lark's announcement, and then Lark came to Mahina and Mooni, "Can I take away Eaglet with me, to show my tree-hole on *The Babool*?"

But, Mahina or Mooni had answered yet, while Raghu rapidly reached to them, "No, Lark, sorry for that, but your tree-hole far from here and it is night time. This eaglet has not any idea about how does find out the way in night or darkness and he will be not able to see or look whatever in your tree-hole in this darkness. It will be in vain, won't it?"

"Oh.... It it right Raghu.okay then, I will come to your tree-hole on the Palsah tree and myself will take him away with me." Lark said to Mahina and Mooni.

"Okay."

"But, I want to say something special and different, " Sugi got ahead and admitted to them. She said and all four gathered bird looked to her, "Why we do call egelt as '*eaglet*' we should christen him with some other name. He is becoming mature and he can fly now."

After then, everybird was talking on this subject only and the banquet was transformed into the Assembly.

"Now, it was about to happen only," Bagga said nurvously to Sona, "Who will think on this subject, to leaving these tasty and delicious foods behind?'

Sona noddd his head and made some voice like laugh. The Moon had gone far from centre and midnight was over now. And it was first time, when one of the great laws of the Vihangwanah had been violated. Becasue, It was midnight overturned and no one bird was still slept yet. It was party time for them. Sona was feeling blessed that, Kaka was not being present there.

This was the beginning of ***July month*** and four or Five days passed out also. In those days, The Vihangwanah Flodded with the heavy rain. Therefore, all coaching classes of Eaglet had been debared. It was seeming like from now rain will fall into the Vihangwanah everyday and that reason The Sun quite paid his visit to Vihangwanah. After the day of the banquet, heavy rain had been falling (into the Vihangwanah) and every bird used to come out from his tree hole, only in search of some food. Lark what said at the benquent that was not completed yet. (He said that he would take away Eaglet with him next day to show his own tree-hole on the Babool tree, but that tomorrow was not arised yet.) except the coaching of flying, there was not another coaching work over yet. Like that, the training class about *stars and planetory reading of Sona*, was incompleted because, of thunderbolts, tempest, heavy rain and cloudy climate. Which story he was to tell to Eaglet conecerning about The Moon. That was flodded away with heavy rain. At the night of the banquet many birds were thinking about, which name ought to be given to Eaglet (They were thinking about christianation of Eaglet) but, everybody thought that, *"eagle",* This name was having every thing on it. (Every meaning) and any other name will not be suited for him, therefore, christianation remained unsuccessful ("It is an eaglet and what name we could give him? one day he himself make his name and that time all Vihangwanah and we all proud of him," Raghu said.). He was talking on last moment of the banquet.

By the way it was not totally right that these all days were totally wasted by rain, when rain stopped for a moment, Eaglet went out from his tree-whole (of Mahina and Mooni's, on Palsah tree) and came back after hovering here and there. He was drenched, because of drizzeling water drops on tree leaves and then, Mahina used to dry up him with cotton -swab. But, when, she was really troubled with these mischiefs of Eaglet and at last he came into the tree-hole with drenched body about eight times. On that time instantly, she huffingly closed wooden-swoop of the tree-hole. But, she quickly had to open it because; Mooni went out to bring Dove. (Dove was the great philosopher of medicins and he was excellent in every type of deasese and illness.) Eaglet got cold because of his wetness and he became harassed because of illness. But, after that, for next two days he only did take rest (Because, Dove advised for rest and Mahina was seeming really very worried.) Many birds and animals (Gilhary and Safeda) came to meet him after then.

But, among these rainy days, the watching duty on Mahina and moon's Palsah tree had not been loosed for a day. Everyday, there were two birds be prerented for the watching duty. On one occasion, Lark himself was present on watching duty on that place. But, untill Kaka or Raghu had not come for this duty.

Suddenly transformation was taken place in the Vihangwanah. Abundent of grass had been there, therefore all forest shaded as a green. After that, new trees were raised there and different types of Vines and Creepers were creeping on land and also on the branches of the trees. Everywhere, fragranted Flowers were introduced and blossomed. Fragrance of various flowers was spreading everywhere. It was really good atmosphere, but no one was happy more than Bagga. He had got plenty of fishes in the river water (receptacle of the river) and he had begun to gift these fishes to many birds. By Sona's opinion the rain like this, had not fallen since many years. And this rain was falling because of only *"auspicious- wings"* of Eaglet *(the auspicious eaglet)*. But, every resident of the Vihangwanah was not happy with the rain, thinking this heavy rain as the auspicious. Safeda- *The big white wild Rat* became homeless, because of rain water had rushed into his residental land hole then Woodpeck made a beautiful tree-hole for Safeda on the *Jamoon tree* along with Gilhary.

Suddenly one day had been dawned (It was really dawned because, previous some days were very black and cloudy therefore, no one was able to see The Sun- Light.). That day was really clear and there was no symbol of rain or black-clouds anywhere. On that day Lark himself went into tree hole of Mahina and Mooni very morning (before his visit, he had given them a *Sound-code--message*). Today he was taking away Eaglet with him in his tree-hole. This wish he had wrecked at the banquet and Eaglet was also excited to watch his tree-hole. Because, he did not see other tree -hole till yet except Mahina and Mooni's one. Mahina and Mooni also permitted for that happily and on the next moment Eaglet leaped on air with Lark. Now, he did know that *there was no any great master than experience was.* He was so happy on his fly that, his happiness had been not lessned a little bit if; he would have flied for whole day and night and onwards. He will fly like this in his whole life. He will remain flying like this from now in his whole life. High..... and ....high......and........more high........

Eaglet relaxed on two places and then reached to outer branch of the Babool tree where Lark accomodated. For that Lark had to give many instruction to him. Becasue, Lark wished that Eaglet did not get hurt by the thorny branches of the Babool tree. Therefore, Eaglet could manage to land on branch very safely. (Lark was afriad about Eaglet's amulet. He knew that - It would be harmful If, the amulet did stuck into any branch.) Lark opened his tree hole - swoop with a gentle push and he got into the tree hole. Then he called out Eaglet in. He was taken aback, as he stepped ahead into the tree hole. He never looked the tree-hole as big as this one. This tree-hole was about Ten times bigger than Mahina and Mooni's tree hole. The rays of The Sun easily came into Lark's tree hole. Lark placed some stones into his tree hole and when Sun-rays fell on those stones, the tree hole had been glimmered (in) with reflected light of those stones.

"These are not prestigious stones But, they reflect light very nicely. These were also given me by Safeda, when I was elected as The President of the Assembly." Lark gave information, "So,this is my resident arragement, How it is?"

On this, Eaglet gave no answer. He only glared at what was present inside of that elegant tree hole. Lark kept two bouquets on there and fragrance of those were lingering inside of every corner. Where, there was, the doorway of the tree- hole, some bunches of wild vines hanging there and their flowers were very nice and strongly essentic. Eaglet was moving his head and trying to see all what was present around there. Suddenly his neak was stopped on one direction and he gone away by that side of the tree-hole. He had seen some thing like big picture. He went more close and now with the help of that reflected light, he was observing that picture, which was carved on inside wood of the tree- hole.

It was a big circle had been carved there and in the centre of the circle there was another circle, but smaller one. In that small circle, there was carved a handsome, elegent bird, who had not been seen by eaglet till yet. That bird was having great *crest* on his head (The sharp crest was shown on his head) His beak was arched and two *Rubies* were set into his eye socket. After then, the big circle was divided by *eight* same straight lines from the small circle and each part was inscribed by a clean out picture of a bird. (Every part was having a picture of a bird). Eaglet had seen many birds from inside of the picture. But, there was something, which was carved below the carved painting. That was looking like something inscripted sentence. But, what was that he did not know really.

"Lark, what is meaning of this symbol and what was inscribed below (under) it?" He asked.

"It is a great emblem of our bird creed and the Vihangwanah. And It is our *'Symbol of Honour'*. It was carved in ancient time and those Eight pictured birds are our main Eight creeds of birds of the Vihangwanah and the small centred bird is our idol. This bird is *a SkyLark* -he is a bird of devine powers."

"Devine powers? Which divine powers?"

"Look eaglet! SkyLark is an immortal bird. He only listens music and his hunger is extinguished by Music only. He lives with hearing of Music and He is very skilled in every type of Music. His voice is great and melodious. His *voice* can stop the time. His Music is very inspired for *dead birds.*"

"What? for dead birds?" Eaglet asked in shocked, "How it could be possible?'

"I also don't know that. The Vihangwanah is the *most ancient* and the oldest forest and from here every thing was started (about birds). In older time, very very old time, we birds had also creeds and reces like, any one bird had his creed very high or one had very low, this. But, one time came skyLark broken it all and he gave everybody an equal rights. But, untill yet some birds are believed in creed. (Creeds are believed also today) That reason the SkyLark is having so importance and greatness. His all powers are great. What divine powers and greatness he contained unknown and hidden for us. Only he knows what he has in his soul."

"Have you seen the SkyLark ?"

"Ha..........Ha.....Ha........ Ha......." Lark laughed on this question of Eaglet.(Lark thought that Eaglet might have connected his name with *SkyLark.*) He turnmoiled why Lark was laughing. Lark ceased his laughing and spoke, "Not I am only. But, no birds have ever seen the SkyLark in his life. It is supposed to be a Myth. There are so many birds, who did not believe in the skyLark. It is only teaching for us. That we have to live with love. It was the message of *fraternity.* Therefore, we shall not differentiat to each other and live with affection. Likewise, you have missed very big thing to see on that symbolic picture. Under that symbol there are two small animals were carved, either side of the picture. Did you not mind on that, did you?"

Eaglet again saw that sentence and this time he looked there two small animals. Who, were looking very peculiar and those were beyond his understanding. He did not understand and asked, "Which animals these are? What is the meaning of this sentence?"

"These animals are *Mangoos* and this sentence was inscribed in old language. That language is diminishing now. And now only some birds can read or inscribe this one. For this language, to inscribe you have to great practice to your beak. And this ancient alphabet is called,

"Half-Picturable Alphabets." I am thinking, If you observe each and everypart of my tree hole, then you can find out more interesting and something and strange. But, before that I tell you the meaning of that carved sentence, which was inscribed below the *Symbol of Honour*.

"*-Love is a only way of the Vihangwanah*"

Eaglet got amazed after heard it, but he did not say anything. He moved on that part of the tree-hole, where he had not obsered cleanly when he saw every part with attention. That time he realised each part of the tree hole was full with the peculiar symbols and inscription. But every symbol were different from each other. Those all were sentences and those had been inscripted in different languages. (He thought that, some birds would have marked their beaks on that part therefore, those various symbols were made). But, now he understood that, those symbols were the different sentences of different language. But now, he wanted to know more. He moved his head back and asked to Lark, Who was looking to him with curiosity, "What is it? and who did inscribed these all?"

"It is also unknown for me? I do not know about it." Lark simply said.

"What?"

"Don't worry! I am not able to tell the meaning of these every sentence. But, I can tell you it s history. This Babool tree is very ancient and historical. Therefore, birds of various creeds used to be reside here, on this tree, my some ancestors also had lived here for some time. That time, only those birds used to live in this type of tree-hole, who was the president of the respected Assembly. Becasue, the president ought to be remain secured by every harm and danger. *(The Babool tree is having thornful branches and that reason. No one can very easily conquer this tree.)* But, common birds used to reside or live in their nests. They did not live in tree -hole like us as we are living today."

"That period was the period of hypocrisy (The period had come with in desguise of hypocrisy) and it was the period of the various revolutions (*In the bird's world*). But, this period gave an ideology about their equal laws and right, and tought us that no one is small and no is senior with his creed, every one is equal. It began from the Vihangwanah and that time who were resident of the Vihangwanah, They took an oath of the unity from that, This honourable-symbol (the symbol of honour) had been emerged and only then they gave protection to small animals. But, not to everyone only them who were their friends and helped them. And after then, one of the ancestor of Woodpeck, incribed this symbole of honour here. And *"We all are equal"*, this sentence, every bird incribed here in their own alphabet and language. But, it is difficult of find out which sentence belonged to which bird -race and from which language. Because, these all languages are not in existance and some of them have been petered out also. And I think, only very rarely any bird might understand these languages in this era. But, I am not able to tell you anything about these languages."

"Means, everybirds are having his own language and own *Alphabet* inscription style."

"Absolutely everybird has his special langauge from beginning of his creed. My language, Raghu's, language of Kite, Sona's language everybody's language is different. Every bird family has his own language and for absorb that languages you have to do deep study and reading and If we became able to learn that all, then we shall be able to familiarize with the culture and life style of every birds."

"But, how can I understand your language at moment?" Eaglet asked with wonder, "Which is my own language then?"

"Look, we did accept a common language for our everyday's life. (and for should be understood by every bird.) Because, every bird can not learn every birds language. It is impossible that everybird can be known about every bird language. Therefore, now our common language is called *"Joint- bird language"* Because, everybird can speak this language. That reason you can easily speak it. Perhaps, your father also used this language therefore; this language can be your own language."

Eaglet now came to realise that, Bird-life has also glorious tradition. Because, his curiosity was increasing. He asked ahead, "These sentences which incribed here, are the only sentences in existance or there some more are exist? Out of your tree hole."

Lark answered on it, "Look dear, knowledge does not have any boundries and knowledge is immortal one. Many places are abundent with these type of sentences left, this one alone. When we see some marks on trunk of trees or inside tree- holes, that time we think, that are only some marks made by incidently or any bird made keen his beak on that part and therefore those marks were made. But, that are not marks only, they have inscribed different types of knowledgeable things or like something that and only we are unkown about that things or stories therefore, we can't understand it. Some birds have inscribed some plenty of amazing things inside the great and dark caves which are very very old and ancient, with the help of their powerful beaks. Now you realise, how oldest our bird genus is! And our Vihangwanah is the part of that glorious and glowing chapter. You would see the oldest trees, about older than Centuries in this forest and also you can see some marks on them like these. But, I don't think that, those marks are understandable for you because, It is very difficult to separate which are marks and which are *bird language -alphabets*." Eaglet never thought that one day he would be acquainted with such type of deep Tradition or Alphabet or Education.

This type of education he would have to absorb in his future. This type of thought had never entered to Eaglet's mind in past. But, now he became interested more and more in this subject. He realised that, it will bebetter for him to take more and more knowledge. It will be advantage for him.

"What happend? What are you thinking about?" Lark asked with looking at eaglet attentionally.

"How many languages you can speak?" suddenly Eaglet asked.

Lark expressed wonder on it but, instantly he recovered himself and imparted, "Dear eaglet, out of from the oldest and ancient languages only one language I know. And with my *own* language, I am able to speak also some *recent* languages."

On this answer by Lark, Eaglet nodded his head and once again he began to observing the inside part of the tree-hole. He had been able to see that every part of the tree-hole was profused with various inscriptions. When, he asked Lark meanings of an inscription, once again he nodded his head negative and said, “No eaglet. That language is also unknown to me.”

“That language is unknown to me also.” Suddenly a voice came from behind them and they both were moved back in shock. They saw, it was Raghu, who was standing their back side, and his various-coloured feathers were glowing in golden sunlight and his body was glimmering in various colours. He came some steps ahead and spoke, “- Becasue, this is not a language or an insription either, I think some president of old time, had been living here, banged his beak in rage so,furiously on that part so, it caused this mark made.”

On this explanation by Raghu they three laughed for sometime.

“Have you looked eaglet? Sometimes happens like this!” Lark said, “On some time, for what we think some mark as a language or inscription either, that is might be not language. But, how are you here, Raghu?”

“What happened? First I had gone to Mahina and Mooni, They told me that you have taken away eaglet with you to your tree hole. I also wanted to take away him with me some where.......but, If..... You don’t mind?” Raghu answered.

“NO. NO. Raghu. There is no problem. I have described him everything, you can take away him with you now.” respectfully Lark said, “Only he has not eaten something from morning now, It is your duty to give him something to eat on your way.”

“Absolutely don’t worry; from now he is in my claws. Take our leave now. If you want him to give some information, once again bring him with you sometime after. Okay! Good bye.”

Lark nodded his head in state of permission.

At the next moment Raghu and Eaglet leaped beyond from thorny branches of the Babool tree. The very moment Eaglet was survived by hiting with a thorny branch.

“Where are we going?”

"Not for any important work or on some important place also.We shall come back very soon because, I have some important work then. So, we are just strolling here and there. Then, you are able to see the various flying ways of the Vihangwanah, and how could be that sought?" Raghu informed to eaglet with getting a gentle turn.

They were flying - ahead and ahead. They were going on from different ways. This side of the Vihangwanah unknown for Eaglet because (He had never come here), Then Raghu took adepted turning through high and high tip- toe of the various trees. He simply sought his ways from branches, from vines and from highted bushes and went ahead. But, Eaglet could not move or turn so easily, therefore sometimes he went here and there and many times, he did have to survive himself from dashing on trees. At last he requested Raghu and they rested on a *"Shalmalee tree"*. On the tree, there was great and intriculated netting of vines and creepers. Those vines were abundent with , *Blue and White* wild essenting flowers, which had been bloomed and they were being swung with breeze of wind of noon.

"Now, I realised how difficult is to fly clean and skilled. How adeptly you could take the turns, while I was not able to move so adeptly." In tired voice, eaglet spoke.

"Hear me, flying means not only flap your wings and ride on air (just it is not only involed into flying.) Then, turn or move rapidly or whirl in air, likewise, speedly get your way from small and narrow branches, to go away with easily from thorny bushes and come down with speed. These all things are the part of a good flying (These all things are involved into good flying.) and these trivial things are also very important one." Raghu gave information.

"But, how shall I learn these all?" Eaglet asked, "You are very very adept and skilled in that. When I shall be as like you?"

"Eaglet, I think you are missing one thing that is, I am some years older than you and therefore, I can do it all and very soon Sona and Kite will give you training about it (and Robin also) and then you will be very adept like me in thise very less time. But tell me? Without the training of flying, which another coaching have you taken till yet?"

"Sona told me, something about planetory and stars - Oh - yes - "*the study of stars and planetory*" but, that class was held before the banquet. He told me the names of stars and planets. But, it was story of old days and I have forgotten lot of things from that. I think I have to study that again." little eagle talked with worry.

"Don't worry about that. Sona will teach you those points again. Now stay here, I bring some fruits for you. Look there down, there is some Bushes over there and they are having lots of Purple fruits on there sprigs. They are looking delicious one. I am going to bring them. Just wait for a moment!"

Thereupon, Raghu leaped down and away with speed of Thunderbolt, his various coloured feathers were shivering with wind and he was glowing like fire glob. Looking this all Eaglet was feeling novelty about his flying and also for Raghu. But, that was not remained for long time. Because how did know a big animal landed by his side with help of hanging on a silver coloured thread and now Eaglet abruptly saw him. He shuddered with fear suddenly. He was not able to think. He even did not know what matter was that? Who was having many legs and uncountable hair on his body? Likewise, He is having pair of forceps in front of his mouth. His two eyes were ambiguous and dusty. When Eaglet realised that the animal was two times bigger then him... He thought about to fly for sake of his life. He spread his wings before the hairy animal reached to him. But, he could not fly. His wings were stucked by something. That thing was sticky, that was net very small and narrow net *(that was spider web)* and it was shining in different colours. For many times, he was trying to free from that but, he did not get success His all efforts were wasted. In that time, the spider had reached so, close to him that he could have given easily any harm to him (eaglet). Now, spider was coming near and near to him and he was beating his front pair of forceps very loudly and Eaglet easily might be imagining his easy death.

- Suddenly, flapping sound of wings came from somewhere and Raghu reached on a top branch of the tree and landed on it . He had brought two delicious fruits in his claws. In very short time, he did note the seriousness of time.

"Raghu save me! What is that?" Eaglet shouted. Adversely, Raghu was very calm and silent. He only once did beat his beak on one another. Hearing that sound spider became silent and he also beated his pair of forceps, which were in front of his mouth for two times. Eaglet did not know, what was going on there. But, those sounds were sounded by him like this -

Raghu - Thack s s s Thack s s s Thack s s s

Spider - Tuck......... Tuck......... kutt....... kutssss........

Raghu - Thack...... Thckacksss....... Thack......... Thassck ......

Thack...... Thckacksss...... Thassssck....... Taassck........

Like that their, "*Thack - Thack" and "Tuck-Tuck*" had been continued for sometime more. But at last the spider walked out, when Raghu said him by his beak -beating. Then Raghu set aside the fruits which he had held in his claws and easily took away eaglet from spider web with his claws.

"Are you all right?"

"Yes. Yes. I did not get any harm from that animal." Eaglet answered.

"Okay. Then have these fruits and eat. These are very delicious." Raghu said with simplicity.

Eaglet was in shock of fear and he was also hungry that reason he did eat those fruits silently. They were really tasty. But, If there were not this type of dangerous and terrible situation, then those truits would have become more tasty for him. His hunger was exhausted now, but his hunger of questions had been arised.

"Which animal was that? So, terrible looking and how did he go back without hurting me?" He asked Raghu.

"He was a *Dark-Spider* and is called *"Hairy"* one also. He was deadly poisonous one. But, he has great medicinal powers in his hair, web and also that poison which comes out from his mouth. But, why he went back from you, I don't know."

"But you both were convassing with each other, (I was thinking) you ordered her and she returned back." Eaglet set his thinking in front of Raghu.

"I was not talking with her, I just beated my beak loudly and therefore, he scared to me and fled away."

"But, why was she also beating his pair of forceps, then?"

"Perhaps, she might be trying to me frightened. But, I did not fear her and she had to bow out herself." Raghu explained, on this explanation Eaglet seemed to be satisfied.

"You are more storager than her so; you could have attacked her and easily run her away. You did not have to be make her frigntened If. There was matter of win and loss."

Raghu had to think for a little time on this matter of Eaglet, " Listen to me, If you could solve your problem with intellectually then, what is need to show your power there isn't it ? Keep this one thing in your mind forever. Now, it will be better to go back."

"But, we were going to somewhere?"

"Sorry for that, it is too late and I have some work at the moment. If, our time had not been wested then, we would have gone some distance ahead. But, it is our bad luck that, we have to go back so early. Likwise, Mahina and Mooni will be waiting for you. Sometime later, I will bring you here with me again. But there is one thing -" Raghu suddenly and seriously spoke, "Ah...... Dear eaglet, it will be better for you and also me, if you do not tell to anyone what happened here otherwise, everybody will be worring for you. Understand there is no other matter."

Eaglet nodded consently on this description of Raghu. But when they were preparing for their return flight Eaglet asked abruptly, "Raghu, but I am still thinking that you were talking with the spider in her language. Are you able to speak her language?"

Raghu did not show any expression on the question. He said calmly, "There is no such a thing like that. (You are just thinking about an impossible thing.) And now mind on the way because you have to find out our return way till your tree-hole (Palsah tree). I shall fly behind you and you show me correct way. Therefore, stop your other thinking and be focus on this matter. So it would be better for us."

****

FIFTH

The evening had turned over sometime ago and stars were peeping out from the clear and blue sky. This was the first time when the sky was full with the stars. (This was the dusk time when stars were to be wanted visible for eyes.) Therefore, before some time Robin had come to Mahina and Mooni and given them message from Sona that he would give the egelt information of stars and planetory .(He would take his class of *"Stars and plantory reading."* Becasue, today's day was very clean, and Sona predected that, perhaps the night also would be clear and clean, So that he could easily teach Eaglet someting about planetory.)

Mahina and Mooni had shown refusal when at first time they heard this message from Robin. Becasue, Eaglet reached to tree-hole of Mahina and Mooni with Raghu, that time afternoon was also to be over. That reason, they thought Eaglet would have been exhausted with that long course of travelling. But, Eaglet was ready for "the class of planetory -reading" and said *"yes"* for Sona's class. Hearing this from eaglet Robin flied back to Sona for the message. Eaglet had raised in his heart fond of studing and knowing more and more about everything. But, he was not fond of to take own experience of everything because, when he was returning to tree -hole with Raghu that very after noon, he tasted savoured tast of *"self - experience."* Because, Raghu asked him to find out the returning away and Raghu was flying behind to him. That time he experienced, what is called to find out the way. And at last, Raghu told him to come after him. When, Eaglet missed his way about of Fourteenth time. Then he reached to Mahina and Mooni and told them what happened. On that Mooni said, "Don't worry about that (you have no need to worry about that. That was not your fault.) Hear, every way of the Vihangwanah is very intricable and also bewildering one. Many birds (or everyone) have to wait for understand each way here because, everything looks like same and every part of the Vihangwanah is much resembled to each other. Therefore, no wonder that you have missed your way for fourteenth times." Then Mooni suddenly made his voice low because of which, his voice will not reach to Mahina who was present at other side of inside the tree hole, "When I and Mahina was newly married, she used to go for collecting fruits in those days. When she went to First time, that time she did not understand anything. She was totally confused and began to cry (she was totally missed, which way go from where) coincidently, Sona and Bagga were flying from there. She asked for help to them and at last they brought her here finally."

Eaglet and Mooni laughed on it silently.

"At the time of night, It becomes very difficult to find out right way here and who has no study of this forest clearly. It is better for him to do not get out from his residence at the Night time. Untill yet today, I or Mahina does not go out from night time and that time also did not come (fall) on us fortunately."

After then Eaglet did not get time to speak some other words to Mahina and Mooni. In quick time Sona had reached there and Mahina and Mooni bid him with rubbing their beaks on his beak. Sona and Eaglet flied away and reached on the *"Khairaah tree"* which was very near and on which Woodpeck carved a great tree hole. (Previous coaching class of *"stars- reading"* was also held here.) When, they both sited down on a big branch. That time The Moon was seeming very big and silver light had been spreadings everywhere. The wind was running very fast and rapidly than that afternoon and Eaglet was worring about on any moment he will be flied away with that rampeging wind. Little sound of babbling - water was coming there and from somewhere, *Jasmine's* slow, intoxicated odour was lingering there with the wind.

"- First, do you remember, what I told you in our last class?" Sona asked.

"Yes- little one I can not remember whole thing. But, I can tell you. Look there that is planet Jupitor which is shining in -" Like this, he began to tell names of the stars and planets. In that he exchanged the names of Venus, Mars and Jupitor and gave some other name to them. Once again Sona made long speech to give him all information about stars and planetory. It was lenghty process but after that, Eaglet noted it all in his mind.

Sona delighted with that and began to give him some information about The Moon and also told him, how light of The Moon is important when, you fly and find out your way and how it helps you.

Then, Sona told him the reason of *'The Night of the New Moon'* and why does Moon make invisible for our eyes on that night. Sona also explained him changes of the shape of The Moon everyday. Atter then, he moved on the subject to the Polar star and told -how would take The Moon and the Polar star (with) centre of flying and find out ways. Sona made a long oratory on it-

"-Look, If you were flying from very high that time you will have to watch on The Moon and from which direction, you are going to checking that, you should come down and observe your shadow. If your shadow is not falling on land, that time, have to make guess on from the Polar Star and identify opposite direction of the wind and think about distance between land, our possition, and The Moon. Then, when every time on our turning point, which is our direction and where is the Polar Star, you have to associate with them and -"

This type of lots of information made by Sona. In that, eye movements was involved and also the movement of the tail. After having heard that all. Eaglet could not understand some point, what was more difficult- to recite this all information or to excute on this all point. Because, he did not understand a word from Sona and Sona also realised that -

"You will not have understood very much from this, I know that. But, practice is very easy more than this speech. But, we shall do it tomorrow. Becasue, I have come to know that you had been out from your tree-hole with Raghu long course of time."

Eaglet nodded his head on it. But did not say a word. Then Sona spoke ahead. "Okay! Then it would be better, if we go back. Wind is also flowing faster."

"But, you are not given an answer of my *question*, which I asked you on our previous meeting."

"Which *question*?" Asked Sona

"I asked you that why The Moon is having dark spots on his surface while, he is so white? What is that? And you were to tell me a story about that?" Eaglet answered.

"Really, I will have to salute your memory. It is great. It was in my mind already. But, I was just examining whether, you can memorize it all or not?" Sona said with whirling his big yellow eyes and spoke ahead, "Hear attentively, It is great story and an interesting one. It belonged to ancient time.Now, I begin the story. *Listen-"*

"It was very very ancient time and was the time of ***"Legends of the Birds,"*** *(This story was a part of Legends of the Birds) -we could call that. That time, was like a magic -era and, that was the time of peace and pleasure. From everyside, on that time thousands of birds were living on various places. Very nice and blossomy flowers used to bloom and those were not fainted away like today's flowers while, those flowers used to be fragancing for many years. There was mountain, on that many birds lived with happiness. There was a family of The* ***SkyLark*** *bird also used to live there-"*

Hearing the name of the skyLark bird, Eaglet's eyes were become bigger in the amazement.

"- Phoenix was his best friend forever. But, he was alone and, He had no family. He was an orphan. Therefore, skyLark's parent supposed him as their offspring. They both had great affection for each other. The skyLark did have the great melody in his voice and he used to sing great songs. Everybird was fond of him. He had the great knowledge of the music."

"But, everyone was not fond of skyLark and his voice. On the same mountain "Agadh" bird also resided. He had great and beautiful appearance. His colour was Golden. He was having a crest on his head, that was colourful and had to change his colours everyday and his tail was long and seven coloured. He was very great pride about his appearance. But, leave his apperane apart; He had not anything to be felt enviable. He used to consider everybody under-esteemate. Therefore, he was not having any friend. Adeversaly SkyLark and

Phoenix had many friends and they always used to give respect to everyone. Agadh was very jelous about skyLark's great voice and he always regreted that he did not have that melodions voice. He did make many efforts to become his voice like skylarks, but that all efforts became futile (efforts were gone in vain.) ·Aghadh's envy was rising day by day with hearing the voice of SkyLark and his praise. At last his anger reached on tip-toe. Because, now everyone neglected his appearance and used to give attention on skyLark's voice. Now, He had to get revenge from SkyLark and very soon, he did get a golden opportunity."

"On one day skyLark's parents ailed very badly therefore, SkyLark and Phoe --nix was in distress and tension. Their worry raised more, when they saw no remedy (medicine) was working on SkyLark's parents. That reason, their health were deminishing day by day. Agadh found out this moment and met to phoneix and skyLark on silent place. He told them that he knew the remedy on this malady. Because, of which skyLark's parent were been ailed, having heard this, they both were be happy and asked Aghah, where they could get that remedy. on their question, Agadh answered, that medicine was present on The Moon. SkyLark and phoenix felt amazed. But they both were very innocent and benign while, Agadh was very shrewd. They asked Agadh that how they could get the medicine from The Moon. Agadh very mindly answered on it that, only Moonlight had the power to produce that medicine and when 'The Night Of Full the Moon' came, that time the power of The Moonlight increased and also on that time medicine became most powerful. Agadh's household was the oldest one and they had great knowledge of medicines,it had to be supposed therefore, SkyLark and Phoenix agreed on his story and asked that how could they manage to reach on The Moon. He answered cunningly that they would have to fly on The Moon with the help of their wings between the time of setting The Moon and rising The Sun. Then Agadh added silently that they ought not to tell this thing to anybody otherwise, anyother bird would be trying to get for The Moon and they both would remain empty. (Meant SkyLark and phoenix could have to come back with empty hand.)"

"After some days there was the night of The New Moon and Phoenix had determined to go with SkyLark on The Moon. SkyLark only told his parents that they were going to bring medicine for them, but from where he did not tell. Afterthen, on The New Moon evening, they began their travel TO The

Moon on leaping from 'the pipul' tree. Agadh was watching this all and he came to know that they both would never come back again."

"SkyLark and phoenix began to fly rapidly when; they saw big bright Moon was became visible in the Sky. They were knew very well that they had very little time and big travelling way in front of them. Therefore, they had to creat great power in their wings and reach to The Moon. They were flying in the direction of The Moon rapidly....... and more rapidly........ But, they could not have had reached near to it. Their wings were flapping speedly. But, their speed had been slowed down. When, midnight had been turned over, they were flying on very high and high in the sky. They were tired and now any time their strenght was to be exhausted very soon. But, they had not accepted their defeat. But, At last phoenix's wings left his companionship and they stopped their flappings. Therefore, he was falling down. But, SkyLark did not allow to fall him down and he held him in his strong claws. On this, phoenix told skyLark that let him fall down and did not hold him because he had to go far for bring medicine for his parents and he could not manage to fly with holding him. But, SkyLark did not hear him and started to flying holding him in his claws.

After long time, The Moon was still on far distance, now he had been seeming at, the time of their flight. SkyLark was now thinking that it was impossible to reach The Moon ever. He knew that after some time The Sun would rise and by that time he could not rach to The Moon. He was so exhausted now, that very soon he also was going to stop his flapping of wings. But, he opened his beak for freshness and began to sing his meolodious song from the beak. His tune was really impressive and so melodious and powerful that The Moon (As per Indian mythology Moon is A God) could hear it as well as every Star and Planet were able to listen that melodious composition. They were engrossed in the music; they forgot their work and their speed was ceased. That reason, the time was also stopped. After some time, The God Moon asked to god "Pavana" (The Pavana is a god of wind who, provide air to the Universe.) that who was singing this great song. The Pavana who presented everywhere answered that two birds were speedly coming upwards in the sky and one of them was singing this song. Then pavana got some more information and told The Moon that they both were coming to him (The Moon) and either bird from them was unconscious, he was fainted and other bird was his friend holding him in his claws.

*And flying upward and singing this song. He also tired now and in preparation of dying on any moment. Hearing this description the God Moon amazed and felt wondered. He ordered to pavna that he ought to bring them very fast to him, with his great power of wind. Because the God Moon wanted more and more about those birds and why they were trying to reach to him. Hearing this word from the God Moon, the pavana released very great wind on them and without taken any hard efforts by both of them (skyLark) they were easily reached to The Moon in a moment. There Moon himself was standing and made their enquiry affectionately and when he asked why they both were trying to come here, they both answered one by one their all story, about the illness of SkyLark's parents and how were they got the information about that medicine which was produced on only sarface of The Moon and could care skyLark's parent from that ghastly malady. The God Moon shown wonder on it and also felt very proud on them and he praised SkyLark and Phoenix. Then the God Moon gave blessed both them that he was going to integrate their appearance in his inner- heart forever and whenever anyone looked to him at that time, he must see Figures of both them on his surface. He blessed skyLark with the blessings that his music would be the top most point of every music. No one could be competed with him and his melodious voice ever. The time would be stopped by his vocal melodious voice and his music would reflect the memories of past for every being. He would have the knowledge of all Ragas'. Then, The Moon blessed Phoenix, who had come with skyLark so far, Though he was on the door of the Death and he had proved that best friend never left his friend alone ever, that his flight would never be incompleted or failed short. His Death would be advanturous one and that Death would bring his re-birth also. The rays of The Sun would not set any harm to him and those always would give rebirth to him. And at last, you or your up-coming household would never be ailed by any dieasese. Then the Moon structured, **"The Ameya parbata"** (The immortal mountain) and forever he located the parents of the SkyLark and skyLark himself on the Ameya parbata. It was happy mountain and always peace there riped. That was supposed to be A great mountain, there time dose not go forward. It is supposed, only those bird could be brought there who sacrifices their lives for others, who try to do good for some one or who wake for everybody's love or friendship. Those bird can get place on the Ameya parbata and they are become residency of the Ameya parbata forever.-"*

" -And now from this great story, you will have got the idea about why The Moon's surface is having that black spots. Those dark spots mean the Figure of SkyLark and Phoenix bird, which have been contained by the God Moon in his heart."

Eaglet's eyes became bigger and his beak was opened. Then he shut it and asked, "But, what had been done with the Aghadh? Who had behaved so sordidly?"

On this question by Eaglet Sona laughed and began to tell," *On that very night Agadh had completed his work very adeptedly. He was over joyed with happinness and in that New Moon Night he was standing on the edge of a lake and looking his beautiful appearanc in that water. Now, there was not anyone as beautiful as him, in any way and very soon he was to be center of the everybody's attraction. But, suddenly a big radiant globe came from the sky and fjopped on him and in moment he was metamorphosed. His body was transfromed in the colour of ashen and black and his neck was become long, his beak became blackish and bent. He had been made big and glaut and clumpsy bird with one contemptible also. His wings made big and queer-one also. His crest, which stood on his head, suddenly dropped down and black hair was growned on that place instead. He and his all cread were changed into the Vultures. That bird is existing also till today as he was in the past. He is never be happy. He has no little bit of kindness in his heart. He is a greedy and glutton one. And he could not be satisfied his hunger, while he eats however. He always looks everybody with his ravenous eyes. He dislikes to see The Moon. He lives on somewhere rocky and arid lands. So, It was the whole story of the Agadh to the Vulture."*

Eaglet nooded on it. He already saw vultures in his past. He had never seen more peculiar and horrible bird than vultures ever. At the moment he could think about that ancient time when the Agadh was looking so beautiful.

"So, is the creed of the skyLark still in existance now?" Eaglet asked, because, only in one day for twice he had heard this magical name first time from Lark and now in the amazing story of Sona. Therefore, he became more interested in this subject.

"No one could tell that. Because, SkyLark was never seen by anybird. How does he look / How is his appearance, It is yet unknown for us. It is just a Myth. These types of many myths are present here only to teach us that don't fight with each other and live lovely. It is the morality myths. Some birds are believed in existance of the SkyLark somewhere and many birds do not suppose it true. But, Phoenix bird exists on the Earth. But, some rare part of land. He lives in some rarest and distant areas from here. But, It is difficult to reach to him. But, the Phoenix birds still have that powers which had been blessed on their by The Moon-God."

When, Eaglet was thinking about it was just story or myth or it was a real life story of the SkyLark, then suddenly. He heard big shout of Sona.

"AHO--- No! The Moon and the sky have been opened so much. How long it has night been," He casted his sight on Eaglet and he was shuddered with that yellow eyes. "Look Here! Because, of your story How been late we are? Mahina and Mooni will be worring for you. Do you not know how dangerous it is? Now, make haste! and fly along with me. Otherwise, you will definitely miss any way of the Vihangwanah in this dark night."

There were many reasons to say that, the Vihangwanah was the most amazing forest in the world. First it was The only bird - forest many birds used to live here, It was very small forest in size. Here, any bird was never Fighting to each other (excluded some exception), then, Mahina and Mooni were very small bird. Although they had taken the responsibility of an eaglet and at the last, lots of mysterious of the Vihangwanah had to be open yet. Like that, there always heavy rain used to fall in the forest. And that reason many works of birds were dragged out. This type of heavy rain had fallen in the Vihangwanah for one and half day once again. Therefore, which fresh atmosphere was spread before one day over the Vihangwanah that was again made dusty and muddy one. And the sky was totally covered with black clouds. Therefore, Eaglet could not manage to fly out from the tree-hole of Mahina and Mooni. That reason, he began to fly in the tree-hole. But, he was not being able to hovering bigger and higher. Because, This tree hole was not bigger than the tree-hole of Lark.

"Dear, don't fly like this here inside, otherwise you will dash on some part and will get hurt." Mahina worringly said when Eaglet was hovering speedly in the empty space and the precious amulet, which he wore on around his neck, was swining here and there.

"Yes, you will be got hurt and once again I-" Mooni also said with worry but, His worry was little different one, "- will have to go to Dove, in this heavy rain with weted body."

Mahina looked sternly at Mooni, on this description. Here with Mooni began to cleaning up his wings - feathers by his small beak.

But, Mahina was worriedly looking up to the hovering eaglet, after having seen this, Mooni said, "Mahina! Do not worry. He is an offspring of the eagle and I heard that these type of adventurs liked by them (They do courageous works everytime.) Now, He is an eaglet and we are the Mynah birds. He could not do any adventure. When his guardiuns will like us because, courageous things are not part of our blood."

Hearing these words by Mooni, Mahina went closer to Mooni, "But, Mooni, This eaglet belongs to us now and now we both are his parents. Therefore, I-"

She did not speak ahead, but Mooni had been running his household about three - four years and now he became very used to Mahina and easily could understand her mind and emotion as well.

"Yes. It is right that at the moment we are his parents and family and (It is right, that) we would be worried for him. But, we could never understand that, How his real parents would have behaved with him. Therefore, we should give him independence but, only in limit, it would be better and you know that *limited independence is the symbol of the progress."*

Now, she was looking, satisfied with the words of Mooni. But, Eaglet was not happy little bit in those two days. Because in these two days, he was to be given coaching of *how to catch Fishes* with pouncing on the water and it was to be given by Bagga. (Bagga was his favourite bird in the Vihangwanah). But, All this programme was spread the heavy rain water on it, and therefore, eaglet had become very sad.

"For how many days this rain still going on to fall?" He asked nurvously.

"Still for three months it will be falling like this." Mooni silently answered.

But, luckily rain was stopped on next day morning. And on that very time in the morning Bagga came to bring him (Eaglet). He had eaten two fruits before some time and he was ready to go with Bagga, for the training of *fish catching.*

"But, it is difficult for him to catch water fishes. He can only fly now. He could not manage that. Would it be not better If he learns other something instead of fish catching?" Mooni thoughtfully asked.

"I know, fish catching is very difficult task one. But, when he leap for catch a fish that time, he would come to know that how to manage fly and how use his claws and how to attack on any running prey or hunt. Therefore, he would be smooth in his flying skills and be able for hunting. It is very important for his life also to understand this all." Bagga answered, when Mahina was rubbing her beak on eaglet's beak.

Mooni satisfied on this description by Bagga and he bid Bagga and Eaglet when, tyey both flied away from Mahina and Mooni's tree-hole in fresh sunlight, from Palsah tree, They had to wish *"good morning"* to Dove and Parinda, who was present on their watching duty on Mahina and Mooni's Palsah tree, from early in the morning.

Eaglet could fly adeptly now. He was studied well for how many times flapped his wings and when gave them rest. But, Bagga was not flying rapidly, having seen it, he asked, "Do you fly with this speed or can you fly more than this speed?"

"Dear eaglet it is not an important matter", when they were flying from above some *Coniferous* trees. That time Bagga answered,

"We know our fastest speed is But, do never to fly on that speed. It is always better that fly on your normal speed. If there is no haste. My original speed is very faster one. But I do never fly with that speed."

It was too old for Eaglet to come on this side of the forest. It was the past, when he once had come here. But, this part of the Vihangwanah was again become unknown for him. Because, the heavy rain of last two days had filled a green and yellow colour in the leaves of the trees, while where land was visible for eyes on that time now had been pervaded with bushes and lingering grass. (Lingering dark grass had begun to Dovede there.) Because, of this grass it would be more difficult to find out the way, Eaglet thought. Now he could see receptacle of the river. It was so filled with water now, that, The Fig tree on which Bagga lived was sunk into the river water, even then that was standing on the shore (of the river). By the one side big hollow was made and had been fulfilled with great water. It was the giant appearance of the river that could only be seen in only rainy season. The river was roaring with his water as like proving her great power on the edge of the hollow, Bagga and Eaglet. In water of the hollow, different types of fishes were jumping and swimming here and there. As like, they were involved in any race. Having beheld this scenario Eaglet was feeling fun with that.

"These all are fishes...... Various fishes and you have to fly on the air and to put your claws on surface of water smoothly, then hold a fish in your claws get out from there and come here to me with the fish, okay ! Then did you understand?"

On this question of Bagga, Eaglet felt very happy and he over nodded his head with over joyedly, "Now, attentively look at me. How do I do that -"

Having stood on both long legs with equal weight, Bagga, then spread his huge wings and smoothly leaped slightly on air and at next moment very speedly but, calmly floated on the water for moment and he lifted up one fish with touching his long legs very lightly on the water surface, he came upward with speed of thunderbolt and once again dropped the holding fish down in the water, from his legs.

"Why have you dropped it down in the water again, while you caught that?" Eaglet asked with wonder.

"Listen, Fish dies If it gets out from water for sometime. That reason fish only can live in the water and we have our one rule that *without hunger we do never hunt any* one. So, you did look it all. What I did and how? Could you do that now?"

On this question, when Eaglet nodded his head affirmative, It looked like about hundread times, he had done this work before in his life. He did not fear to the gushing water of the river - But, he also did not know why he did not fear to that tremendous force of the water. [It was also wondor for him.] Because he had never seen so, furious stream of the water in his little life. But, he was ready to everything. Because, he was part of the eagle family .Bagga also amazed on this courageous behaviour of Eaglet.

"Okay, then do stand on your both legs, with equal weight, make your wings stable on both side. Look, Fishes are very slippery one and they easily slip from our claws therefore, do catch it very tight in your claws and catch one of small fish, it would be better for you. Okay? Fly now-"

Eaglet flied on the air, with thinking on about all instructions of Bagga. He went vey high. He could easily see *Silver fishes,* which were swimming in the water here and there. He selected one fish which was on the surface of the water, with aiming on that, he speedly dived downward. But when he reached to very near on the surface of the water, he could not control his speed and also his wings. He did not stop himself on the time and he plunged into water with the fish. Whereupon, Bagga instantly leaped in the air and lifted up Eaglet from water with the help of his two long legs. Eaglet had been totally drenched and also drank some water.

"Okay. It is okay. It is better attempt." Bagga was consolating him, "At least you managed to rod on the fish. I also could not perform this feast yet. Tell me, what happened?"

Eaglet shaked his head speedly and moved his neck, Thereupon, his amulet was also shaked and it's centre piece (The Rubi) shown in The Sunlight.

"It is really difficult. At first, Fly high in the air, then dive downword speedly with being stable your wings. After that, move your claws correctly and in angle.Do not distract your attention on from, that fish, which on you have aimed. And on that, it is difficult for me to stop myself surface on the water. I don't know, how do stop myself in the air, without flapping wings. Therefore, I have committed this mistake."

Bagga laughed, having heard this and said, "Hey---- It was not a mistake dear. It was your first attempt that reason, it was to happen certainely, when, I was your age and gone to first time for fish - catching that time,my targate also missed many times. So don't mind for that. Now be ready and try again."

Then after having dried his wings, Eaglet was stood on both legs and spread his wings. He once again leaped into air and targeted on one fish, Now he was rapidly coming down and next moment when he was about to lift the fish from the water, suddenly-

Zapaaack -ssssss

once again Eaglet totally surrendered into the water and after coming on the water surface, Bagga caught and placed him by the side land. At this time he had been drenched by feather and feather. He had a cough. He shook his body once again, when his dry-cough was stopped and looked at Bagga with questionable glance.

"At this time, you came very fastely down. If you are going to coming down with so, high speed then, you would have to catch fishes, which are deep in bottom instead of surface of water. Come little bit slowly try again, this time you will definitely do it before that, I go and show you once again."

Bagga spread his white big wings once again and went on high and dived. He made steady his wings, he smoothly touched his long legs on water sarface and cought a rustling fish in his legs and dropped it again in the water. He returned to Eaglet and stood by his side.

"Did you look, it is an easy task."

Eaglet nodded his head very energetically and saw that even, the long legs of Bagga were not touched by the water. Now he was full with energy looking that all he knew he was an eaglet and courageous one. He leaped on air and became steady his wings and fastely began to come on that fish, which was jumping in the water. Eaglet was full with confidence. Now, he could do anything. He spread his fingures of his claws and reached very near from the surface of the water-.

Zapaaack -ssssss Zapaaack -ssssss

"Once again." some time later Bagga said, when Eaglet's second try was also gone in vain.

-Zapaaack ssssss-

"Again-"

-Zapaaack -ssssss-

"Now, it is last one, concentrate on your targate, you can do -" But, Bagga's talk was remained incomplete -

Zapaaack -ssssss.......gooood. ......goooood...... goooood..... gooodooood

His mouth was totally filled with water. And by the next moment he was held by Bagga, in his long legs.

"Okay now, it is lot of for today. you did better." At last Bagga said, when the little eagle was dried up.

"What was better?" He asked to Bagga in frustration, "I was not become able to catch a fish at least a once. Contrary, those fishes were enjoying the game of jumping."

"But, listen, before some time you straigtly were falling into water, but now you can stop in air little bit and - then fall, it is a progress, isn't it?"

"Yes, that is right, But, one thing happened because of this practice, Although I could not catch a fish at least once, Even then, my swimming practice has been easily prepared here and one thing yet more -" Eaglet sneezed and said, when they were preparing for their Flight (towards the Palsah tree), "I wish that the watching duty of Dove might have not been over till yet because, I will have to take the medicine on my cold once again."

It was a long and borring treatment on the cold, which eaglet got from his fish catching class. (Where at he weted many times in the hollow water) and therefore, till now Eaglet had not been stayed in the tree hole. So long, ever. Dove's opinion was about the cold of Eaglet that, it was the strong cold and therefore, he sought out some medicinal plants from very distance and made the medicine with them and gave it to Eaglet. It was so horrible in taste that after taking the dose of thethat medicine, beak and throat to be burning for some time. (And also used to numb for little time.) And over that, this programme was to be procceded for Nine days more. Dove strictly warned Mahina and Mooni that Eaglet ought not go out from the tree hole and let not allow him to be wet in rain. After that, visiting for Eaglet, there was made haste by birds. It's looking like a queue.

"How did he get so heavy cold suddenly? I am thinking, he was going for the class of fish - catching, was't he ?" Mahina asked to Bagga, when on next day he had come to meet Eaglet again.

"I thought he had gone for to learn a swimming, without that, there was no reason for him to drenched so seriously." Sona, who had come with Bagga said.

"He was being taught that how to catch fishes absolutely. But, he could not stop by the time, on from water surface and that reason.he dived in the water about Seven times." Bagga described all.

Many birds and animals (Gilhary and Safeda) had come with some fruits for Eaglet. Safeda who had the calibre of make the medicines from planets and shrubs. (Safeda was very adept in to recover accidental injuries.) He had come with a great little fruit namely "*Golmol*" and when he gave it to Eaglet, then he had to say it's name to Mahina and Mooni also and that it was an excellent medicine on cold and fever of any kind.

Lark had come to visit Eaglet and returned back very quickly some day's before and he got with him vocal message from Raghu. Who, could not come to meet him (Eaglet). His message was -

"I could not come individually, very very sorry for that. Recover quickly and begin strolling here and there once again. I am hoping that, next time you will be able to catch one fish at least. Otherwise, there could be need of Dove once again. Best of luck."

"It would better to do stop the class of fish catching. If again there would have been need of Dove's help." Eaglet thought, when he was told to take the medicine of Dove by Mahina.

But, Kaka had not reached to meet Eaglet by any form. He had not sent any message or not present there either. It was fourth day But, Kaka had not shown his black face there. Why he did not come, Mahina and Mooni knew very well. Kaka had been opposing Eaglet from the First day of his appearence in the Vihangwanah. And now. it was overturned one and half month although, he was not transformed with the view about Eaglet. (But, why had he helped to Eaglet for teach to fly, It was the riddle for Mooni, Mahina and Kite also and because of Kaka's *obstinate* request, they had not told that to anybody. But, even then how had Raghu happened come to know it, that was the biggest mystery for the three of them. But, though Mahina and Mooni intentionally thought that because, of the heavy rain he (Kaka) might have not come perhaps; on other side, other birds had met Eaglet as their covenience, with weting in heavy rain sometime or with reposing on the branches of the trees on their way.

But, today's night was somewhere different one. Never experienced by the Vihangwanah before. It was so heavy raining at the time that it was seeming that whole rain over the world was trying to fall only on the Vihangwanah and Never exprienced lightning and thunderbolts were being thundered on there. Every tree was shaking with the roaring of the thunderbolts. Therefore, any bird might have not stept at the moment, in the Vihangwanah it was certain one. Everytime, the tree-holes and trees shuddered with lightning and thuderbolts as like, tree was to be fallen very soon. (Every time with thundering and lightning an illuson was made that water in stomach might be stirring.

"Why, are thunderbolts lightning so horribly today's night?" Eaglet asked to Mahina and Mooni. His central piece of the amulet was hardly shining in darkness.

"Certainly, something will happen evil one!" Mahina fearly said. When Sky roared loudly again.

"It is just a superstition Mahina," Mooni explained her and then he answered to Eaglet, "Dear; today had been cloudly weather all the day perhaps, it is the result of that. Therefore,sky is sounding like this."

"Then, any thunderbolt can strike on this Palsah tree also?" Eaglet asked. Mahina closed his eyes and nodded her head. There was totally darkness into the tree hole.Although they could look each other ambiguosly with the shining of the Ruby stone, which was a central piece of the amulet that was worn around the neck of Eaglet. Mahina was thinking that, it would be better if Eaglet stop asking this type of horrible questions. But, thereupon Mooni opened his beak-,

"Listen eaglet, till today, No thunderbolt did strike on the Vihangwanah ever. But, no one can make decision when, there are thunderbolts like this. "

"Look Mooni, could we not converse on any other subject instead?" Mahina requested. She was fearing with thunderbolt and lightning.

"OH God........ Dear eaglet your *moth-*" following words of his own sentence, Mooni adeptly swallowed. But, untill Mahina shockingly looked to him, "- *Mahina* fear to lightning theefore, we speak on other subject Okay."

Having remained silent for sometime suddenly, Eaglet got an amazing thought in his mind (heart) that he had come in very different world without any preassumption (and he had been made very lovely by every resident of the Vihangwanah) But, one bird had been very near to him, and at the moment he had totally forgotten him. But how, could he forget him, that one was his father, he had totally forgotten to his father. He had been so engrossed in other things that he unattentionally sacrificed rememberance of that bird, who was his father.

Dadaam - ssss Dhudumssssss goodoomss goodoomss

No bird of the Vihangwanah perhaps like as his father, so energetic, so white incolour and so elegant (powerful and smart one). But, where did he go? At first he was thinking his father would come very soon and then he also could go with him on that native place where he was born and would get coaching of how to fly.

-Dhudumssssss Dhoodoom sssssss

But, now it was too long and he was become enough old and mature now. At the moment he was getting knowledge of various things. But, he had been not his father who was giving him that all knowledge, while thay all were strangers and unknown one and they were not even bonded with blood relation.

-Dhudumssssss-sss-Dhudumssssss-ss-Dhudums

But, they all had proved that there could be one relation, which is superior to relation of blood. *Relation of Love, which do not have to sustain on any other relation.* That is completely independent one and the supreme. It always helps you otherwise, why these birds of the Vihangwanah, nursed him. Why they gave protection him so highly and also why they so hard worked on his practise and coaching perhaps. These all could not have done even by his father too, did he have so information. Was he adept in planetory reading and star reading like Sona was? Was he able to study ancient alphabets or languages? was he skilled in carved these type of tree holes? Could he fly like Raghu, or could he easily talk to anybody in his language like (Raghu)? or was he adept in medicine and curing the maladies like Dove ? or was he able to search priceless stone's and Rubies like Safeda did ? Answeres of all these questions were hung in air somewhere and that would to be never answerable for him. He had ceased to make all surmises about it. He knew where was his father gone?

-Dhudumssssss-sss-Dhudumssssss-ss-goodsssgoodssss

Where he was gone, perhaps all birds called that place as *"Ameya- parbata"* (immortal mountain) Where died but, kind bird go after their death. It was preassumption of birds. But, he also did not know whether it was interesting story or a true one. But, If his father was not part of the world, so definitely he was resting somewhere in the unknown world for a long time because, he knew that his father was very kind and lovely and perhaps this time with the help of this thunderbolts and rain, he was trying to tell something to him.

-Dhudumssssss-ss-goodsssgoodssss

It was peculiar and strange to thinking like this. But why he was thiking like this in this stormy - thunderbolty - and rainy night (which was being stirred with storms - thunderbolt and rain) He did know that he could have thought about something blissful or mirthful except it. But, this stormy night had collected all sombre thoughts in his mind. Just as, only drop of the rain was being collected in the river water at this time. He did not know either Mahina or Mooni slept or were thinking like him with closed eyes. But, he was certain about they were not in sleep.

-Dadaamsss Daddamssss Dhudoooomssss

But even then everybody loved him here, at the Vihangwanah and was helping him with their bit's. Bagga was for him as like his father. Although Mahina and Mooni were very near to him and his heart; Sona's eyes were very penetrating and strange (yellow) big one but, his heart was transparent and kind one and he had knowledge about everything. He did not have any idea what was Raghu knowing but he used to seem strict one. Dove had come his help, when there was emergency and wanted of his help. "How much Safeda loved him!" Its symbol was hanging around in his neck as an answere at the moment. Everybody loved him although; everybird did not come closely his contact.

-Dhadaam - Dhudoooom ssss- Dhudooomsss

Kaka, who was black with colour and now seeming with heart also. Why was he so angeed with him, this question was still an unanswereable for Eaglet. Even then, he helped him to teach his first successful fly. But why? Why Kaka had come himself to him and taken away him for his first independent fly. These all movements *(black movements)* of Kaka were beyond his imagination. Perhaps, Kaka must have been some evil plan in his mind that time. But, because of Kite's persence (which was taken placed sudden) therefore, he might have not done something danger with him, Eaglet thought it all and that reason Kaka requested (with solid breathe) Kite that did not tell to anyone about that; But, after that day he had never shown his black face to any bird (and any part of the Vihangwanah also). But, why he was thinking this type of incident. Yet, it was just unbelievable for Eaglet.

At the last he remembered one sentence, which was spoken by anybird or somebird had read it from the *carved incriptions* either.

"If your thoughts are hearing of your heart, with overcoming on your brain then, it could be supposed that your thinking is indepdendence totally."

Dhaddaaam - Dhudoooomssss- Dhudooom

The morning, after Three day's was not so cloudy, as much previous Two day's and nights were passed over. but ,even a tree was not harmed, Although, the rain was so heavy one . All trees were standing as it was. The river water was flowing with lapping over the both shores and there had no any sign of the Bagga on the Fig tree, which stood on the river shore. He might have gone to any friend bird *(might be to Sona),* for rescuing himself from ailing again because, of so heavy rain. Though, any tree had not been fallen because of heavy rain but, it was the season of blossoming of the various fruits and some trees were loaded with ediable flowers and now that all washed out because of the heavy rain of previous some days. And it was a big consumption about foods for everybody (They had to tolerate it.) But, there were very few birds who was *vegetarian*, in the Vihangwanah. The sounding of the various living - creatures had been increased in the Vihangwanah. Therefore, birds like Sona and Bagga were in jolly mood.

- For Safeda it was impossible now to walk on paths or land. Because, there were lots of streams of dusty water flowing here and there from every path and secondly, there was mud everywhere either. That reason, Gilhary gave him all information about *"the paths of the tree branches"* therefore, he also began to trevel from trees. But; it was a long procedure for him to go with the help of tree brances so, in this type of state, he used to leave some works and responsibilities on Gilhary and she too, happily accepted that.

Safeda was not able to walk or run on wety branches adeptly. He had not his leg's and nails (on legs) alike Gilhary had therefore he saved himelf from falling down from a branch of trees many times.

The eget had flied out, in the early morning. Before he went out, there was a long time arguments between Mahina and him. But, he told in outspoken words that he was feeling better now and he became enough adept in flying now. He could fly better therefore, he might fly alone and there did not need to come somebody along with him for watch over him. But, Mahina had been worried with tension and tried to stop him some how (in the tree hole) But, when Mooni casted a indecative glance on Mahina, she became silent and Mooni permitted Eaglet to go alone out from there with words *"Come soon."*

"He has not been so adult yet and how does he know about flying? Just from one week, he could fly something better, and he recovered from deasease just two days ago and he got out from here immediately today-" as Eaglet closed wooden-swoop of the tree hole, Mahina did bomberment of words in resentement on Mooni. He was silently hearing her words, "How could you give permission him to go alone, Mooni? This is horrible time and Weather changing within in little time. You know very well, how much Vihangwanah can be horrible in the days of rainy season. On every second various types of Shrubs and wild vines grow up here and which path is known for us, that is made unknown for us on very next moment. Many times, many birds have missed their ways, lots of time they have to take help from other birds. I myself many times missed or forgotten many paths when, I was new here and Eaglet is very small yet. He exhausts after travelling on some distance and now at the moment he is all alone. Look Mooni, we are his parents, and we can't desert him on the air. How did you permit him to go out from the tree hole? He is our *offsp-*" Mahina closed her beak and stopped her talking, But, Mooni already understood what she was to be say ahead. He went closer to her. Unflown tears had been shown in her eyes. He placed his eigher wing on her back and said, "Mahina, he is not our offspring. You are only his- rearing mother and I am guardian for him. He is now being adult. (He is trying to sharp his flying skills). For how many days shall we keep him lock into this tree- hole with us yet? At first these all days of his life are very imporant for him, all these days are learning days for him, learning the out-side world . But, becasue of these dreary days, and rainy one he does not fly or not go with any other bird to outer world. He is not able to absorb any type of knowledge either. Our love is very supreme for him I know that and even I knew that you consider him more something than your own offspring. But, we are those small birds of the Vihangwanah, for them adventure mean, to bring some fruits from long distance. We are very less in our flight. We do not fly thousands of miles. Neither we wet in water or drench in the rain, we are just for ours. But, he is Eaglet, the offspring of the eagle. It is that bird, whose every flight contains a great adventure, his least flight reaches to the Welkin and power of his wings can take him to every corner of the world. His beak is as hard as diamonds and can break anything and he catches snake in his steely claws and could chop him an uncountable pieces. But, we can not do any thing from these, because, we are not the eagles and we are also not able to give anything from us to him without our love. But, I know that how much love you can bestow on him, his own mother could not have given him so much. Therefore, don't worry about that sometimes, he will have arguments with us. But, that time we shall have to show our broad mindness, although we are very small with our size. But, never be growing small with our heart one. Do you understand it?"

On this, Mahina nodded his head. She used to feel pride on Mooni and because of his decision making power, she had been tempted by him and also married him, "Mooni, your speaking is the answer of every problem. But, it could be harmful for him to go out alone any accident might be happend to him do you know better, Mooni? You had to go with him." She was looking in eyes of Mooni, in where her reflaction was standing. On from this she experienced what she was for Mooni. But when Mooni laughed she amazed. He said, "Mahina, now after some days, I could not fly with him we both are. His speed will be developing day by day and he will very soon be able to hunting. Therefore, I could not fly with his speed furthermore. So, I do one thing, I see who are on the watching duty at the time on both *khairah tree.* I will tell one bird from them to go behind and watch over him gradually. Okay? "

Mahina nodded his head and Mooni speedly went to closed wooden - swoop of the tree hole. He came out. One-one birds was present on either khairah tree. One was Parinda and other was Woodpeck. Mooni said "Good morning" to both but; he was become very glad to see Parinda there. He said to Parinda, "Parinda, you must have seen that Eaglet was flied to somewhere before little time ago. Look. He is all alone. He argued with Mahina and me and told us to do not come with him. Now, you go and search where he has gone. But, only do not let him realise that you are chasing and keep tracking of him. Only watch over him okay?"

"But, why you let him went away alone?" Woodpeck shockinlgy said, "I thought that he went some where to Bagga or Sona for his coaching?"

"Listen me, he wanted to fly alone because, he had not been flying from very long time. Therefore, he argued with us for long time and went off. Therefore, Parinda please go back to him and help him, If he misses some way -"

"But where and from which direction did he go?" Parinda asked in haste of flight.

"You certainly will have looked that, go from that way where on he flied and search out him in any case but, do not tell to any bird about it."

"Look Mooni, The Vihangwanah is very small but, it is intricated and very cofusing one. Do not allow him to go alone again like this .I go and chase him."

"Thank you." said Mooni.

After a turning, Parinda obscured behind the huge *Gulmohar tree.*

"Mooni, don't take tension, Parinda know every way of the Vihangwanah like (that) it is a mape which is present in his tree-hole. He will very easily scent him up." Woodpeck said in confidence.

Mooni nodded his head, he knew it very well that each mysterious path, oldest path or confusing one, had been easily travelled or trodden by Parinda once. He had the greatest knowledge about every paths. It would be supposed unbelievable if, anybody said that he knew more paths than Parinda. And because of this rainy season, various types of shrubs and trees were grown up, therefore, many birds (adept in searching the correct way also) have to change, many time their routine ways too. Mooni now remorsed on his decision, that why he was permitted Eaglet so easily. Now, suddenly he coasted the price of Mahina's feeling. But, even then he was great belief on Parinda and also his capability.

The Sun had been trying today for revenge of previous Three days. He was giving Three day's hotness from early in the morning today. But, Clouds also were not ready to defeat, they were coming again and again in front of The Sun and it was seeming like, The Sun was playing hide and seek with them. But, no one was eager to watch it. It was long time turned-out to The Sun rising. The elget and Parinda also had been disappeared from long time. But, neither one from them came back yet. Therefore, Mahina and Mooni were pacing up and down in their tree-hole, on the Palsah tree.

Thereupon, there came the flapping sound of the wings and the very next moment, the wooden swoop was opened and Eaglet entered in the tree hole. His white feathers were disturbed with wind. But, he had a fruit in his beck. He placed it by side and he began to glance at Mahina and Mooni. Who, were looking at him like, he was a stranger.

"What happened?"

"Why Parinda did not come with you?" Mahina asked, because she was told by Mooni that Parinda had gone with Eaglet (For the searching of Eaglet.)

"No. but, I was not gone with him (Parinda). Why were you asking for Parinda?" He answered them and after some time he came to know all. he was seeming amazed, "had you sent Parinda after me for watching on me?"

Thereupon, Mahina and Mooni looked to each other. "where had you gone?" Mooni asked.

"I had only gone out for exercise my wings, which were not even moved from many days. There, I saw a beautiful tree of beautiful fruits. I ate some fruits there and brought this one for you (both). And also on that place I happened to meet with Kite, But, he suddenly became disappointed with me. But, for why I did not know? he did haste and left me here and very quickly flied somewhere. But, he was frightened with some thing when he saw that I sited on that perticular tree and eating fruits. Perhaps, he angreed because, I had gone very far and alone from here?"

Hearing this, quickly Mahina and Mooni went closer to the fruit (which Eaglet brought.) Looking the fruits, eyes of Mahina and Mooni were goggled.

The fruit was the having Purple colour and Red speckles, same as in size of *Jujube fruit.*

"This ..... This .... fruit, where from did you bring ?" Mooni inquired.

"That is very distance and long place from here and I think, it was the only tree there. By the side of that tree, there was a big tree too. Thornful and biggest one."

"But, how did you reach here so, quickly from so long distance?" Mahina asked.

"Yes, I can fly enough better now."

"Were you seen by anyone there? Mean except Kite."

"Not at all, Kite might have seen me. I was to stay on that the beautiful for long time, but Kite was in hurry." Eaglet gave all information, and Mahina and Mooni stared each other is shock. Mooni speedly stepped on the one part of the tree-hole.

"Where are you going?" asked Mahina.

"I give *sound- code- message* to Parinda that, he was reached himself here safe and sound." Mooni answered and knocked his beak for four times on special incarved inside part and it sounded -

Tuckssss Tuckssss Tuckssss Tuckssss Tuckssss

"That mean, you had really sent Parinda after me?"

Sound- code- message was resounding till, Eaglet asked. Mooni nodded his head.

"But why?"

"Because, we were worried for you and we always worry for you. Not only we but, every bird always worry for you. Therefore, we did take this step. If your mother and father (parents) were in our place, they also would have done samething for you." Mahina said with getting more closed to him, "you are not our offspring, I know this fact. But your protection and responsibility is only aim of our life."

"I talked you very bad this morning. I think your every decision is right. I thought on your every word, when I was flying. I really wrongly behaved in the morning so, I am sorry, very sorry for that."

Having heard it, Mahina became very emotional. she said, "It is just needless to say sorry, Dear I was trying to obstacle you here too much. So, It was my mistake, I realised it later."

"Now, please close this shop of forgiving to each other It was a past that what happened one. It is okay. But dear promise me one thing that,you will never go to that side again,of the Vihangwanah."

"But why?"

"Because, that was the horrible part of the Vihangwanah and very long from here. That is profused with poisonous plants and shrubs and therefore, it was forbidden area for us. There is not good anything. Otherwise, you are paremitted to go everywhere but, except that one. we also not go there." Mooni said with spread his one wing front and Eaglet placed his wing on it very quickly, "Okay. I am taking an oath that I will never go to that forbidden part ever even by the mistake also-"

- But, the last words of Eaglet did not sound correctly. Because, all Vihangwanah was resounded by sound-code-message and Mahina and Mooni heard it with attention.

"Oh......it is time to say Good bye to you both." Mooni shown haste and said, as the resounding was stopped.

"But-Why- Where?" Mahina said.

"This sound-code-message was for me. It might be for the important work (one). so, I have to go- " Thereupon, Mooni was gone out , from the wooden-swoop, he stopped for a moment and peeped inside the tree-hole and said, "Do not go any where to leave Mahina alone here, untill do I not come again." After then, he leaped on air and obscured in yellow, flowered tree with an elegant looping around to the Khairrah tree.

"What's mean by sound- code- messsage?" Eaglet asked.

"It is a sounding message, some time of message with sound. That contains some thing mysterious for somebody. Every bird has his own sound- code -message. That sound is produced after knock your beak on the special part of inside the tree-hole.. Everybird uses his own-special sound-code-message and about that anyone do not have any information. It because, only that bird, for whom the sound-code-message is being knocked, can identify it. Now, which sound-code-message was knocked sometime ago, for calling The Mooni. That even I could not recon, I also did not know that sound- code- message was for Mooni and he will be not sensed, If any sound-code- message is knocked for or from me. But, if all bird will have to gathere on any place, suppose for a banquet or Assembly meeting, that time the *common-code-word-message* is knocked and everybody have the knowledge how does it use. Everyone knows the meaning of *common-messaging- sound.* Therefore, any bird or animal could be called out any time." Mahina told him.

"But, when I will be able to get the study of it all and when I will use it?" Eaglet questioned, hurried.

"Very soon. Dear, These all knowledge about sound-code-message has been given us by Woodpeck and only he will teach you all about this. But, when your beak will be strong and hard .We all would have not been thought about sound-code-message, If Woodpeck was not being here." Mahina answered and carely looked to Eaglet, "He will teach you all, this soon. But, yet, you have to learn a lot."

"Okay. But why Mooni went there?"

"OH----- I also don't have any idea about that. It is only to be known when he come back, untill we eat something a bit."

It was afternoon and the time had been changed into the fornoon. But, any bird had not come yet to bring Eaglet with him for any coaching or training or any educational class. Therefore, he was in deppression. Thereupon, Mooni aslo had not been come back yet (and whereabouts of Mooni yet to unknown.). Eaglet was again and again grumbling and complaining-

"How beautiful and clean was the today's atmosphere! And also there was not rain whole day. Although no one bird has come to pick up me for my class. No Bagga, No Kite, Sona or Raghu either. How is it possible, today's total day was wested. It is evening time now and this time I could go with only Sona for the study of planetory and stars."

"Perhaps, you have been a *leave* (holiday) for today, from your coaching and training." Mahina said in the tone of consolation.

"But, my previous some days also were wested by heavy rain, and I could not go for my classes (coaching) and why they will give leave to me for today? What is the reason?" Eaglet asked, "-They would have said me, If they were going to give a *leave* me"

On this question, Mahina did not have any suitable reason and also answer, she only nodded. After some time, night fall and all Vihangwanah was swallowed by darkness. Eaglet was in asleep, after when he aet Barry with Mahina. But, Mahina was still awaken The Moon was hidden behind the clouds even then, Mooni was still to return. After that, Mahina had to wait long time for Mooni and then he came in the tree hole with the softly pushing to the wooden-swoop. He kept the swoop open. Therefore, the ambiguous Moonlight ought to come in somehow. His feathers were very badly disturbed by wind. as like, he was attacked by someone.

"What happened Mooni? why had you been so long? and who had sent that message-?"

Mooni sustained himself. He moved his beak on his disturbed feathers and said, But, before he guaranteed that, Eaglet was in deep sleep.

"Mahina, that sound-code-message was knocked for calling me by Lark. He had gathered the Assembly in his Babool tree-hole."

"What? The Assembly and also I have not been invited?" Mahina utttered with wonder.

"That Assembly was not for everybird. That was private one and only I ,Raghu, Kite and Lark were presented for the meeting and you could not have come because, Eaglet would remain alone in the tree hole.The matter has been very serious-"

"Which matter?"

Once again Mooni looked on Eaglet and spoke, "Raghu and Lark were worried because of Eaglet's behaviour. They just asked how it was happened, how Eaglet had gone to that forbidden part of the Vihangwanah and alone one. On that I said them that he was not listened to us and got out from the tree-hole alone with in fury. But I told them that It was totally our blunder and I said *"sorry"* to them for the mistake. I also told him that Eaglet had given me an *oath* that he would never go to that forbidden part again in his life (even not look there.) On this Raghu felt enough consented. then, Raghu said ahead that Eaglet could have been hurt or injured by something or could have fallen in some type of danger. But, Kite sent back him on right time therefore, everthing was happened correct. But, now Lark placed responsibilities on us that neither let Eaglet go alone somewhere or not get him angree."

Mahina nodded her head positively.

"They proclaimed that Kite, Sona and Safeda will collaborately give him the coaching of *hunting*. If weather will be clean enough like today's."

Thereupon, Mahina who looked firmly at Mooni for some time and did not speak a word.

"- And I think, there is no need to tell you more about when any small bird become adept into hunting and what have to do after that?"

At the moment, Mahina's eyes were appearing inanimated. She did not nod for sometime. But spoke later, "Every bird have to get that experience in his life and his parents also. I know very well when offspring gets his *first ever hunt.*"

Mooni nodded his head and moved for closed the wooden-swoop in a one stroke.

The afternoon of Next day's, had been clean and weather was better. Then wind began to flow fast. But, there was no inclination on of bad weather or beginning of the rain either. Sona and Kite had come and taken away to Eaglet with them some time ago. Because, from today his real coaching was to begin. He was going to learn how to hunt any animal (any animal). Therefore, they were going towards *the big Banyan tree,* which stood on the river shore. That land was isolated enough and there was not plenty of trees and was free atmosphere for the training or waching on Eaglet too. They were very soon landed on a *Sheesam tree*. Eaglet now was be able to fly along with Sona and Kite wings to wings.

"Look eaglet! Hunting is one of the important phase of bird life, out of the important *Three phases*. Therefore, it is hard one but easy also a bit. But, after then you will be able to live your life totally independent and without any sustain. (*It is one of the right in bird life which is given after own adept-hunting.*) Therefore, anyone must be perfect in hunting." Sona gave total information.

- Suddenly, from the surrounding green grass, and flowery one began to sounding like *"Khusooorsss Khkusooorssss."* Eaglet being able to see that, some thing was running through the deep and thick grass and very next moment a white big swab was got out from it. He was a Safeda- The big white wild rat.

"Good afternoon Sona! Afternoon Kite!" Safeda stood below *'the shisam tree'* and said with looking upward, that time his head had been totally bent on his back.

"You too Safeda. But, you are being little late." Kite told.

"Because, of rain the land is so muddy and wety yet that, it is impossible to run or walk on it. I totally weted when, I was coming through the grassy field." he shuddered his whole body and some drops of water were spattered around, and said, "So, everything is ready?"

Eaglet wondered and asked, "WHAT IS READY?"

"Listen, you will have to catch Safeda, through when he is running. He will be your hunt. Therefore, you have to hold him in your claws. Becasue, when you go on your own or real hunting that time, you have to do same. you must catch that animal in your claws." Sona imparted him description of all things.

"What? But, if Safeda do get harm from me -"

"Don't worry about that. Because, it is about to impossible that Safeda will be caught by you. Because, he is so fast and runs so rapidly that, for you it is quite hard to catch him in your one flight and untill there is the matter about his hurting -" Sona said satisfactorily, "He himself is a great doctor of every accident and injury. He has the every type of remedy on it. Therefore, pounce on him without any tension or worry."

On these words, Eaglet shook his head. He was going to do that work for which his wings had been shivering.

"Safeda, run ahead then Eaglet will chase you Okay." Kite ordered to Eaglet.

Thereupon, Safeda started to run very rapidly. "Glimpses of his white tail was sometime appearing here and there. Then, Sona said Eaglet, "Go eaglet and catch Safeda, *"best of luck."* Sona and Kite collaborately said.

Without saying *"thank you",* Eaglet spread his wings with full energy and flied on air very soon, flying on that way on which way Safeda had disappeared in grass. But, Safeda gone very far and sometimes his white tail lightly appeared in shrubs and green leaves. He was running so repidly that, Eaglet felt wonder that how could he run so fast.With his tiny legs. He tried tofixed his aim on Safeda and began to flying so speedly that, yet now he had not flied on that speed. He dived down and flying on some distance from land and grasy - shrubs. He was going ahead smoothly and speedly. Therefore, he had to come up and down to miss from the lashes of shrubs and tree branches, so causing many times Safeda was being disappeared from his eyes. His Amulet had pulled back in the air. (Swinging here and there into the air.) He became able to see glimpses of Safeda's white colour on some distance ahead. Therefore, again Eaglet contained power in his wings and went ahead speedly. Now, Safeda slowed down his running speed and he was to be caught very soon by Eaglet but, suddenaly-

Zaaapaksssss -

Eaglet shot into some heavy brambles, which was very front to him, like arrow, becasue, Safeda turned around so quickly that, Eaglet could not realise anything. He quickly got out from the bush (luckily he was not harm ghastly.), some leaves were getting stucked in his pricelesss amulet and his feathers were got disrupted. He instantly leaped once again. He already determined that from which way Safeda might have proceeded. Therefore, he was begun to fly tremendously. After some time he saw Safeda was running from green-wetty-grass. This time. He also increased his speed and got his claws ready. Now, he became ready to pounce Safeda again. But, once again Safeda stopped himself very quickly and turned above. On this time Eaglet was to dash on the thorny bush ahead. But, he saved himself from that bush very hardly and with a whirl, he turned back.

"*-So for because of this reason, Hunting is the importnat phase, in those three fundamental basic phases -*" He - Eaglet thought in his mind. He was tired now and his wings were become weighty. Because, Safeda was running on so intricated paths that, Eaglet had to do his speed low and fast everytime and had to turn for twicely. Although, his eagle blood was rustling in his body and ready to prove that, his hunt did not have to go long distance from him. So, he could not do anything. He went on high with thunderbolts speed. Wind was dispearsing his soft and white feathers here and there on that hight. He made able to see a white point which running from green grass. Eaglet jeted his speed more and more fast and he flied exact on top from Safeda, some distance ahead and stopped himself on air with flapping wings, it was very difficult one, but he had to do it. Safeda was running ahead, because he was not able to see Eaglet, but when he saw him, he stopped his running and tried to get turn back from Eaglet, but it was too late to do anything for Safeda, when Eaglet glanced that Safeda was stopped, he resumed his fly as speedlly as winking of eye and pounced Safeda easily with his rocky claws. But, Safeda yet did not accept his defeat. He was trying to get rid from those claws. But, that was the claw of the eagle and it is difficult to imagine if, any thing is caught up by that then that could be never realesed by that claws ever. Safeda was enough weighted to lift up. But, he leaped up once again with Safeda; after collecting suffice strenght in his wing daringly and began follow that direction, where Sona and Kite had sat on the branch of *the shisam tree.* He reached to that tree very soon. It was a very charming scenario. The white eaglet was flying with holding the white rat (Safeda). Sona and Kite were looking to them very wonderly as like they both were seeming something strange. But, Kite has a different saprkles in his eyes. Eaglet kept Safeda on the same branch, where Sona and Kite had been siting and he landed safly on the branch.

"You did it? And proved yourself as an eagle. Very good!" Kite uttered with enthusiasm.

"Safeda, have you really been canght by Eaglet?" Sona asked with unbelievely.

On this question, Safeda waved his head but in nurvous mood, and said, "Yes, it is true. We lost the bet."

"What? Which bet?" Eaglet questioned, who was panting yet.

-Kite smiled and said delightly, "Look, Safeda said that you would never able to catch him in your first attempt and Sona also agreed with him. Therefore, Sona was to give me eight fishes and Safeda was giving me food for two days and if you had been not able to catch Safeda then, some fishes and fruits would have been given to them by me also. Now, you won and I can fly in air with the help of happy wings. You are great eaglet; you have shown your tremendous power."

"But, Safeda you can run so fast, even then how were you caught by Eaglet?" Sona nurvously asked. He was disappointed.

"What do I tell you?"Pantingly Safeda began to tell, who was drenched because, of water drops on the grass, where from he had been running," You both are not able to fly like Eaglet, he can fly faster then you both. His only one leap is enough for me even then, I saved myself for two times. But he chases so speedly that, even we can not surmise his wings or flying speed. His wings do not make any sound and today, weather was little cloudy that reason his shadow was not falling on the land. Therefore, I was not able to guess his correct position. But, I tell you one thing. After some days no one will able to compete with him in his flying from our Vihangwanah. He flys very speedly, If you not believed, test him now Sona-" Thereupon, Sona and Kite looked to each other, "when you used to play the *game of chasing* that time, you also will have not caught, me so, instantly. His dive from the Sky is so fast that........I could not describe that in words. He comes as fast on land from the sky as a meteor."

"I can't believe your description Safeda, are you telling true?"

"Really, what I said now that all is correct and true."

"But, when he flys with us, that time, how can he fly with our normal speed then? why he does not overtake us?" Kite said.

"I don't know that, but when he is chasing anything with his heart, that time he fly tremendously" Safeda answered.

"Suddenly, how did you begin to fly so speedly?" Sona asked to Eaglet.

"I was flying with my natural speed." Eaglet gave explanation. "But, I think when I chase anything, that time my speed is naturally developed. Now, I caught Safeda! What is next?"

"Ah........ We shall come here later some days that time you will have to do this work again, to catch Safeda. Likewise, you don't have any need to guidance further more. Because, you shut up our beaks. I think we both should take guidance from you about hunting. We are also bewildered from seeing that, how could you catch Safeda so. Quickly infact, how could you hold him in your first attempt? We come here after some days, and you will do same practise okay." Kite spoke, "Let's go Safeda, I drop you to your residence."

Kite held Safeda in his steely claws when Safeda bacame ready for flight and jumped on air from the branch of *the Shisam tree.* Then Sona asked to eaglet fly behind him and then Sona himself leaped into air. That time, eaglet was grudging, "But, this was not setisfactorly performance for me, I was shot into bush once and for second time-.........."

On from top of a *Birch tree,* Kaka was lookin them to flying off. Branches of the tree, were swinging by wind, Kaka's eyes were fixed on Kite and Safeda who, had been caught in Kite's claw. Having looked this sight Kaka laughed with contemptation-

"How does Kite not feel ashemed, when he touches mean and frivilous animals like Safeda? He should think about his creed and supreme status little bit. I am thinking that he also came lower step as like Lark one. Probably, this eaglet had to compel everybird to step down from his high status. But, that's nun of my bussiness. OH God! I will prefer rest into my tree-hole than, become obbessed by these parvenu- "

Kaka spread his black wings and began to fly smoothly. But, opposit side from that path, *from Sona, Kite, and eaglet had been going-*

Next some days were the most hectic days in eaglet's life. when from he had pounced Safeda with spontaneous chasing power of his wings, from then his life's each day was going rapidly and not boring one but, As like those day's had been simply flied off with invisible wings.

("For what I did pounced on Safeda so easily and why caught him so quickly? What would have happened if I had not done this?" These types of thoughts had been coming in his mind from before some days.) In fact, rain had shown its kindness so over that, it was not fallen a drop in those day's. Therefore, he had been badly attacked by every type of coaching and training, Becuase, he can smoothly fly now, that reason every one supposed him adept in flying. Therefore his all coaching had been begun sternly. Safeda and Dove were giving him information and knowledge of various thees and plants and shrubs. Among them some plants were having the medicinal powers. Bagga was practicing rigorously from him about *Fish-catchaing*. But, at this time he did not fall into river water but, he was not able to catch an alone fish too. Similarly, Sona and Kite again and again telling him to catch Safeda faster and more faster. (Quicker). But, this time, he was proggresing better and better and on the one time, he got lift up Safeda in some seconds only, but, this time Sona and Kite did not bet. On another hand, Gilhary was giving him the knowledge about how to find out hazards when walked on the land and through thick bushes also, from which bush he had to beware, she was telling him. He felt wonder when he saw Gilhary was running more speedly than Safeda. Although, she had not been taken for hunting practise instead of Safeda. He thought on other side, he had been become crezy by Robin. Robin's flying speed was the best in caparing to other birds of the Vihangwanah and therefore, he might have been used for conveying messages, Eaglet was thinking. (Robin was a small bird that reason, he could have had his way easily.) The whirling into air as like Robin, to get way from the narrow places and to land on branch with great speed. Eaglet had never seen practicals like these in his life. Robin used to whirl on the air and disappear in moment. Eaglet got failure, when he tried to himself turn around like Robin, when his speed was about *hunderd percent* lower than Robin. He could not even chase Robin at once. (He granduarly bet with Robin to fly twice, but Robin used to cover up half distance, before his (Eaglet's) beginning of flying.) He had become divotee of Robin's flight. As like, he did like flying of Raghu. But, still Woodpeck had not interested in his coaching about "How use the sound *-code-message.*" and he even did not take any coaching class of Eaglet (Woodpeck had not shown any type of hurry about it.) Sugi also had not shown any haste about her coaching. *"How weave the nest." ("Untill beak does not get enough mommentum, While there is no use to learn about how to weave a beautiful nest.")* But, in these days Sona used to tell something deep things about stars, planetory or planets. In these day's there was not cloudy atmosphere for a moment and all stars and planets used to seem clear and clean. Therefore, Sona was giving him the information about new stars and planets. Eaglet was getting mad with reciting the names of *supreme stars* and he was suffering from the totally forgetfullness about those names, at that time Sona became disappointed and used to say, "It will be difficult for you if you begin to forget the names of principle stars or planets. You will have to keep it in your mind for more some days. Otherwise, it will not help you to fly at night time. Afterthen, It will be okay that, you will forget these all names (because, you will have an idea and used to about to fly at night), But, at the moment you have recite, the colours, the positions, of the stars. Otherwise, this all practicing session will go into vain. Very soon, Woodpeck will teach you writing a language (Inscription.) then on that basis you might memorize it, with the help of writing on the trunks of the trees; therefore, you will be able to read it everytime and get it in your mind. But, at least, at the time you have to print this information on your mind okay-"

But, that was very difficult to remember. Some plants and medicinal vines have the same strange names like the stars. Therefore, names of the medicinal plants and some stars had having resembling names. Therefore, sometimes he used to tell plants name to the stars and some time gave stars names to medicinal plants. He always confused between the name of *'shattaraka' star* and *'shatavary' plant.* Therefore, sometime Sona used to bang his head with his own wings and some time, Dove bang his wing on his own head. But, yet Koel had not begun his teaching of singing. Because, she thought that The complicated subject like Music, eaglet could not learn easily. But, she was interested to give him introduction of various natural instruments of the Vihangwanah.

He had to go for three different types of hard coaching for everyday. Although, the coaching of *"Airy-hunting"* had not been begun yet. (To abduct hunt from any flying birds.) It was a relaxation to Eaglet because, after that, his condition might have been complicated one. But, in spite of which coaching was going ahead at these days, that was very tiresome too.

"But, why my coachings are continued to so late night. I have to face three-three various trainings at everyday. Why are you trying to give me these all knowledge so early in my life, why you all are showing so haste?" On one night when, tiry eaglet came return from his coaching, that time he asked to Mahina and Mooni.

"Yes. Yes. I also agree with you and can easily realise your troble, enough is enough now. Mooni, why do you not say something on it? Had you also worked so, hard in the as same age of Eaglet?" Mahina said furiously. That time, she was parting the disturbed feathers of Eaglet because, his speed was also become low because of that disturbed feathers and she was looking at that *wound* which was visible on his one wing. Mooni afraid when he saw Mahina was so furious at moment, but, then he recovered himself and spoke, "Look Mahina, you know well about the condition of this time and these all coaching is a part of security of Eaglet. It will help him for always and even his parents also would have taught him all these, If they were here. So, it is an important education for him and this time is right for that." On this Mahina and Eaglet were made somewhat satisfacted.

"They are going to teach me carving language or alphabets, after some days why? Eaglet questioned, it was dark night now and with today's heavy coaching sheduled, he was became very tired.

"Hear me dear, when you accept any language! At that time you have to accept the culture of that perticular language," Mooni told

Eaglet, when he placed his either wing on the back of Eaglet, *"Language comes no alone ever, but every time language brings its own culture with her. (Language comes with its culture).* Understand! Therefore, when you began to carved our language with your beak, that time you could be able to understand the culture of and tradition of the Vihangwanah.

"But, what is the importance of that?"

"Even I don't know also. But, I think you will get enough advantage from that language. Because, for you it would be better when you learn how to produce sound-code-message that time, this type of practice of carving language will give benefit to you. Now, it would be better, if you go to sleep, tomorrow morning you have to go with Robin for another coaching class. So, this disscussion we shall continue tomorrow okay!! So, "Good night" Mooni said with closing the wooden-swoop of the tree hole. There fore, inside of the tree-hole was hidden into darkness, becasue The Moonligh was obstakled by the wooden swoop, from coming in.

For very long time the wind had been flowing as it was. The Moon, which had hidden behind the clouds, now comes out with smily face. Though she was half as like, she was smiling on those clouds, which had not been successed to cover up her continuelly. It was long night time and dark one, and the scented flowers like *"Jasmine"* and *"RatRanee"* were squandering their fragnance on wayward wind, and wind was delivering it in every part of the Vihangwanah. Uncountable inscects were murmuring around that various flowers. Raghu was flying in this long night time and seeming calm. (He was flying from very high in the sky.) The wind was flowing through *"Bamoo thickets"*(Reed-thicket) with tremendous power and when wind went from hallow-bamboo's, it was sounding like the tone of *flute* and symphony. At a time, wind was going through endless Reed's therefore, anyone could hear many rising and falling tone's of flutes. This bamboo thicket was present at different and distance part of the Vihangwanah and only Parinda lived by side of this part (only Parinda was a resident on this part.) But the thickets were quite away also from there. At this place, the leaves of various Trees were flapping on each other. It was sounding sweet. Raghu smiled in his heart; He wondered to saw that Nature produce so sweet music and she herself appriciate for her own Music too. Raghu knew very well that many species which exist on the earth do not have any trait of this type. He was still hovering in the air and hearing the elegant music of the nature. Though, river water's sound was not sounding here very loudly, but it was attuning with the music of bamboo like any *"Tanpurah."* Thereupon the sound of flapping wings was heard from the distance, a white glob was coming near and near. Raghu very easily realised that was Parinda who was glimmering in silver colour below The Moonlit, He was coming to Raghu straightly.

"OH Raghu, how are you managed to come in this part and so dark in the night?" Parinda now was flying along him asked; he was glimmering more and more.

"Parinda, there is only reason, for me to present here, I never leave any chance to hear this type of natural music. It helps to do empty your brain again and again and feel pleasant." Raghu said and asked glancing at Parinda, "But, what are you doing here in so late night?"

"I am not here to do some work. I can hear confortably all this musical sound in my tree hole and it helps me to sleep thoughtlessly. The music is the magic and it can happen anything. But, I am looking you after many days? Where you had been so, long time?"

"If I did not see by you, that's not mean I might not have been seen by anyone. I was present at the Vihangwanah and was busy in very important work. I thought, you are very well known about, *'The important Responsibility'* at the moment?" Raghu asked with stabled his wings. His quills were dispersing by the air and he was seeming volatile. But, Parinda was serious, as like, The tone of *"Puria Dhanashri"* or *"Todee Raga"* might have been Resounding behind him. (*Todee* and *puria dhanashri* both are serious and sombre sounding Ragas.)

"Yes, you are busy in the deep work, at the time, everybody was into his own work and it is strange that they have their work. So why I have no any work, that why am I still empty? Everybird everyday flies here and there all the time. Everyone has taken responsibility of Eaglet. I have only duty to watch over on the Palsah tree (of Mahina and Mooni's.) But, after then I totally vacant and sit in my tree hole without any work and look to other birds, who are having lots of duty. Only once Robin had came to me with the time table. But, after then I have no responsibility of any kind. Give me some work or I thik that I am not able to do any work or task for the Vihangwanah. Therefore, I have not been charged any kind of responsibility." Parinda said, his voice was disappointed but, not furious or full with anger. Because there was no use to angree with Raghu. Raghu did understand everything and everyone. Everybird had the place of honour or respect in his heart for Raghu. Raghu for a moment glanced to Parinda, now wind was flowing great and fluting of Bamboos and flapping of leaves were rising and rising higher, therefore, Raghu spoke loudly over the musical sound, " No one dare to say that, you do not have ability to do any work. Not Lark himself too. You have proved yourself very important for us in the past and present also. You were very close to Kaka. When he was the president of the Assembly you have great relation to everybody and everybird knows that every path of the Vihangwanah was very well known to you and No one more informed than you about secrets paths in the Vihangwanah. Many times you have found out many birds, who were mistaken their ways. When, there is matter about your work, then, you are the greatest dectectiveand mystery hunter in this forest. No one deny it therefore, that work only probably for you from many years and everyone know it's very well. And even you want any other work, and then wait for some time because; you will have to give detail information about every part and secrets ways to Eaglet. Therefore, you will have great responsibility on your shoulders in the future. Don't forget it. Actually, we have no truely liable taks for you at the moment, which I could hand over to you. Therefore, which work will be given to you, be ready to accept that."

Parinda nodded his head. He was flying some distance ahead to Raghu. Becuase, Raghu was bigger than him about three and half times. Parinda asked, "There is any bird workless like me?"

"Yes some are satisfied to be remained empty. For that I can not do anything. Let keep it behind. Koel still do not have any work but after some days she is going to do *introduction of music* to Eaglet. then there are Woodpeck is workless still, because, his subject is very hard and one Kaka also!" Raghu said with simplicity.

"What happened, does Kaka not have any work?" Parinda wonderly asked.

"No. No. he has great work for him. But, he is not ready to accept that. Do you know very well, how strictly he does hate Eaglet? Therefore, he prohibited himself to (do) not fall into *"that type"* of work. No one could be made ready him to do that work. Many birds want that no work should be handed over to Kaka about Eaglet." Raghu implored with slightly flapping his wings.

"That is right. He is the strangest bird of the Vihangwanah ever experienced. He is not black with his appearence only but heartly one. But, he used to hear me, when he was the president. He was very friendly with me. Although, I and he is very very different in the colours-" Parinda said with little smile.

Raghu nodded consently and said, "Kaka, hates white colour so that, The Moon hates equally to an eclipse. But, how did you manage with Kaka?"

"It was uncertain question for me too. But, he used to love my decisions. That time he *was* my friend."

"You *were* friends, it is not true. You *are* still friends and still he can hear you." Raghu spoke to look at Parinda. They were flying on that pollard of the tree, on which leaves were flapping like claps. Parinda glanced at Raghu, with questioned look.

"Gooroom Kooroom sssss goorkoowu mooorss gooorooor."

Parinda said something like this and it was his native own language. Raghu did not keep waiting to understand it. But, he had to ask for the meaning of this sentence, "What are you saying?"

"Ignore it Raghu! But, what do you want to do from me. I don't think, he will listen me now. I voted against him in the Assembly.

Therefore, he could have been angree with me. so, what do you expect from me (to do)?"

"Do not lots of thing. Do just Kaka prepare for the coaching of Eaglet only." Raghu said, as if he was informing about the night's atmosphere. Parinda stunned after (hearing this) and he dashed on tip-toe of one tree and managed to go ahead through it.

"It is as difficult as to be born a crow in colour of various coloured parrot." Parinda said when he assured that Raghu was serious, with pleasantment, "But, what is he going to teach."

"Oh! I also did not determined, what will he teach. But, it will be better if you try once." Raghu requested.

"Okay Raghu, You know everything and think well. Therefore, I will definitely do try for you." Parinda meekly spoke but, he had not bit of confidence in his words, "But, it is not possible."

Raghu nodded, "But, attempt is the first step towards the success." He said.

"Gooroom Kooroom sssss goorkooww mooorss gooorooor."

Again Parinda uttered something in his tongue. Raghu did not get anything.

"What did you talk?"

"Leave belind it But, I have to go now." Parinda spoke. "I am pleased to speak with you Raghu. Call me without hesitation, if there is some work for me any more. Okay then, now I leave, Good night." Parinda whirl into air and flied away from there. Raghu was glancing him for some seconds. Still wind was flowing rapidly here and there with whistling sound, wind was gushing now and tune of Reeds had reached to its highest point and along with that leaves, branches also rustling very horrible. But, Raghu remained to hovering there then for some time. He was slowly moved on another side and going away and away from there. When he disappeared totally from there, suddenly wind was stopped itself, the flapping sound of the leves ceased and the Bamboo thicket, which was playing various tune of flute before some time, was stumpped suddenly and wind was obscured like that, it was never flowing through the leaves and the *Bomboo- Thickets* ever.

****

SIXTH

August month had been turned over more than half and everything was begun changing in the Vihangwanah. At the first hand The Sun was begun to shine brightly and the percentage of the rain had been deminished. Even then, Eaglet was troubled by daily practise and coachings. Although the rain was more less than month *July* one but, the cloudy climate was always been present for welcome. Everybird was accenting of the training of his own subject. Till now Eaglet was adepted into *'catching the hunt'* and it was his lovelist feast (comparing to other.). But, every training section was not loving for him. He could not memorize lots of name of the various medicinal plants and hurbs and the names of *Twenty seven stars (Nakshatra)* was so weighting on his mind that, he used to be every name here and there, and which were not names of the stars, that also he used to tell Sona. and also he told that name of stars to Sona that were actually not name of any star (Nakshatra).

"Not *Megha,* it is *Magha* star." On one night, when Eaglet mistaken four names of stars that time Sona said, "properly mind on it. You have to learn this now-"

"But, what is need of these stars (Nakshatras) for me?" Eaglet asked nurvously.

"Look. The Sun always revolving through The Zodiac with the help of these 27 stars (Nakhshtra) and also The Moon one. Therefore, it is helpful for you to know about The Sun and The Moon closely. Therefore, every species and animals are rellied on it. Not for only birds but also for *Human -"*

"What is mean by the human?"

Sona thought for a second on this question and imparted, "Human being means human race, human is an animal, but not totally, he is more than animal. He is having two legs, two hands. His brain is more perfect and powerful than any animal or bird on the Earth."

"Is he having wings like us?" Once again one question thrown by Eaglet on Sona.

"No not at all." Sona told, "He has not wings but, even then he can fly. He could do anything to gain, what he is not having. Although, he was the supreme human being, he loves to behave like rude animals. He doesn't want what he has ever. *He has a big heart but, always he acts like heartless creature."*

On this description, a strange one, Eaglet looked at Sona, with great wonder. Sona, know very well that, Eaglet had never looked any human being in his whole but, little life. He asked ahead, "Shall be I able to look him ever in my life?"

"Perhaps, on any auspicions occasion luck will bless on you and will show you the human - animal. But, it is very difficult, because, this Vihangwanah is far-far away from the human- locality. So, that for many upcoming years would not have to become mighty to bring any human being to the Vihangwanah. Therefore, If you do fly very very long Abroad from here, then you could be able to see any wondering human beings. But, he has not any special thing to look at him."

"Did you see him in your life time?"

"No, Never ever, I heard only his description." Sona straightly answered.

"If he is having so powerful brain then, he will be a brilliant one?" another one question.

"Absolutely he is brilliant. But, the Nature does not allow that things, which he has without knowledge and brilliancy either."

Eaglet shook his head and stared to Sona for a once. he did not determine to ask the question or not, but, even he opened his beak and asked. But, with muttered voice.

"It he like *Kaka?*"

Thereupon Sona began to laugh. He stopped his laughing with great difficulty and spoke ahead. "No. He is not alike Kaka. Kaka hates only you...... Okay! Now stop this questioning you could not have any help for your flying to discuss about on human beings. Therefore, leave him behind and tell me, what will happen and you will interpreate, If those Three stars come into a line.......... " Sona pointed up his either wing to the sky and asked.

Along with the subject of *Stars and Plantory reading,* Eaglet was very bad and back in a subject of Dove. That means *"Medicinal Plants and their uses."* it was more difficult than the subject of Safeda. But, Dove was never angreed with Eaglet and If he did commite hundred mistakes, even then Dove explained him without an annoyance. Dove was the Philosopher of medicinal plant which cure the various type of maladies. Therefore, names of deseases and also the plants were very difficult. But, though, Eaglet was ever eager for to attend this class. They both were standing by the thick bush and it had been numerous flowers and crest of Red colours, it was emiteting hot odour and how this hurb used to cure a cold, Dove was giving information about that in this class -

"In previous month when you had been troubled by cold. That time I had not got these flowers. Therefore, I used these leaves for treatment on your cold and made pills from them. These leaves are not too good and effective, its odour is hot and burn throat when you gulp it. But now look at these flowers-"

Dove stretched his neck and pulled off a thick Red crest. Then, he gave a petal from that into Eaglet's beak, he chewed it, it was sweet and sour, it was tasty one, "Now, you saw, it is sweet enough. If these flowers had been available that time and made pills from it, you would have taken that happily. But, that was not seasion of these crets-flowers. Now, you got an idea that if you have cold, you easily could rely on this evergreen shrubs for any time. But, don't worry about that, you would have no need to prepare any medicine, Until, I am present here." Dove laughed.

"I had come here with Safeda some days ago. That time he told that roots of this shrubs are used when you got wrecked, any perticular part of your body like wing, neck or, clows. Suppose If you wrecked your legs, that time you have to envelope (Roll on) these roots into the same leaves of *the Evergreen hurb*. Then, tie it on your leg which is wrecked, then, you would get comfort very soon." Eaglet told with confidence.

"Might be. Safeda is a philosopher (doctor) of injuries and accidents and when I was injured with my eigher wing that time, he provided great tretment on it. Therefore, at the moment I can fly so smoothly. I am happy to see that, you are concentrating on your education very well. May be Safeda is a great teacher." (Safeda will be teaching really well.)

Eaglet nodded his head and asked," These type of treatment is known by every bird?"

"No.No. Not at all." Dove said shaking his head with impatient, "I have got it by my ancient family. Everybird has not knowledge about it. Therefore, I am always called, when if something deasease or malady is there, for a treatment."

"Then, why you are giving this knowledge only to me?"

With this question Dove became something worried. But, he recovered his voice and spoke, "Look, you are an eagle and the eagles have to survive in very different places. Therefore, he knows every treatment and measure. Therefore only, I can teach you these all and Safeda also. If some evil accident happens to you, you ought to recovert yourself gently and therefore you have to fit it into your brain."

But, there was a big question about how to get it into mind, Woodpeck even had not started his education and he had not taught him alphabet too. He still was also not able to produce sound-code-message, but, he was progressing in Robin's subject day by day. He flied with Robin, he came to know how to transfer weight from one wing to another, and he had been learning very subtely with time. This coaching class and *fish catching class* had become favourite classes of his. Bagga did not instruct a little bit now and he used to teach everything with merrily. At last, one day he dived in the water so well that, without touching to the water surface, he caught a elegant fish and finished off it on a tree branch. (Manage to get off his beak on the fish.). Bagga was very happy that on moment and told him that his education would have to proceed for some days more and then it could be stopped.

When he used to come return the tree hole at the night time then Mahina and Mooni, ask him what he was taught that day. Then, they made long reciting about his education and then he went for sleep. Mooni and Mahina used to tell him various stories about their world and sometimes, they canvassed on what is important for the life. When he returned to Mahina and Mooni that time he felt feeling sustain as well and he slept with silence.

In these Fifteen day's, there was no rain at the Vihangwanah though, the elegantness of the Vihangwanah was not lessened. Whichever, shurbs and hurbs had grown in the rainy days, they were still greenish yet and the river was flowing as furiously as it was flowing in previous month. But, night's atmosphere was not cloudy one, other hand it was very clean and pleasent and every star used to seem clearly. Wind was also as tickle as previous days and with same tramp like on from top of trees.

That was the month of rainy and *Autumn* together. It was too late to over turned the midnight. But, suddenly, the wooden swoop on the Babool tree was opened and Lark came out from it. He casted his sight as far as he could. There was no other sound except the river flowing water and if left behind shaking tops of the trees, there was none to visible under the blue sky that was overflowed with dazzeling stars. Lark closed his wooden swoop and he rode on winnowing wind with his wings. He was going ahead to against the direction of the river. This area was crowded with trees and he was flying by side of these trees. He flied on from Mahina and Mooni's Palsah tree Then he flied away top from the tree of Koel, and began to flying to that green and elegant Taramind tree, which was became visible to eyes now and standing on some distance. The tree was older than Two hundred years and standing elegantly with the help of his mighty and giant roots. The wind was little faster on this side, therefore, the branches of *the Taramind tree* was moving like a blade of sword. Lark had to manage himself to keep protective from those aggressive branches, which could have broken him into two pieces with one blow. He landed on the big branch, in front of that branch. There was a closed wooden swoop in the trunk, Lark went ahead and knocked it with his beak and called out -

"Raghu, this is me, Lark..."

There was a opening sound of swoop (wooden) from the inside and it was opened soon, but, it was not Raghu, who came out from inside, he was *Kaka.* Kaka looked at Lark with spited eyes and said, "Good night, Lark."

"What are you doing here at the time -." Lark did not answer on Kaka's greetings, but, asked him, "Where is Raghu?"

"OH... I am here, inside. Come inside you both." Raghu's voice came out from inside.

"What was your work with, Raghu, Kaka?"

At once Kaka opened his beak and laughed bizzarely, *"Kasska ssss kasssskasss kassk,* Nothing Lark, Just I wondering here and there, suddenly I sighted Raghu, and he called me in his tree-hole and we chated. Because, now I am not the president of the Assembly otherwsie, I would have flied like you here and there in the night time."

"Look Kaka -" Lark said angreely.

"Let avoid it," Kaka said without hearing Lark, "I would have never disfouled my creed, my race, because, of an eaglet and decision which you have taken about him, to stay in Vihangwanah. I know your feelings. No one do not easily let slip out his presidentship because of-"

"Kaka - "

"Kasska ssss kasssskasss kasskss Kasska ssss kasssskasss kass

Once again Kaka talked something in his own tongue and forwarded some steps from the wooden swoop of the tree hole, "Don't stress yourself, Lark. I go now, I have some important task also, not more important that you have, - Raghu is waiting for you inside, give me bid and also very Good night for you. Bye-" without glanced on Lark, Kaka leapt away from the branch and soon disappered in darkness on a some distance ahead. Lark entered inside, moonlit were coming in the tree hole and was reflected by those stones which there placed by

Raghu. The tree hole of Raghu was also a bigger and there was great and lots of carvings inside there.

"Where is Kaka?" Raghu said, looking Lark alone came inside the hole, and came to Lark.

"He just zoomed off. Did you hear our conversation?" Asked Lark, Raghu shook his head on it, "Why is he so angree with me. I have been elected by the honourable Assembly members of the Vihangwanah as the president. I always behave with him humbly, talk meekly, even then, he behaves me like as I am a prisnor or accusor. He has been against me everytime I do not know, what my fault is."

"Hear me, he had been the president of the honourable Assembly before you and every president is the president for one season. But, It was his bad luck that, he was not stabled as the president for the whole season, but, he was supposed to be egostic and by him some decisions made wrong. So, the Assembly members majoritily knocked him out, held election again, and that time you were elected as the president. Now, tell me who will endure so much insult. Then, when he was president that time, you were opposing him on his every decision and point, not only you but, some other birds also. Therefore, there is no wondeor that now; he is affronting you on your every step." Smilingly Raghu said.

"But, listen to me, I had never objected him, when he had been the president, but, I was every time setting out my opinion for only to do one's good. Unfortunetely, it was always against Kaka, so, what I do for that and for that reason -"

"-He was dethroned away from the presidentship, and you have been elected for it, right?" Raghu completed Lark's sentence, Lark nodded on this, but he looked disappointed. He spoke in very serious voice, "But, whole Assembly had elected you for the presidentship, although, you had not been interested for that place ever. Then, you had implored the Assembly that they ought to give the presidentship to me."

"Yeh, It was right,"Raghu stably said, "And They all accepted you happily as the president of the Assembly. Weren't they?"

"But, actually not by everybody?" Lark complained in heavy tone.

"Listen me Lark, nobody ever get full of popularity, and when everybody behave with you appropriately as your status, that time it is better that anybody should have to your opposit side, this is my own thinking. Then, you have to be room to progress yourself more and more." Raghu explained gently.

"But, your story is different Raghu. Though you do not have any special post yourself, but, even then, everybody..... means everybody totally respect you. You are loved by everybody. No one in your opposition, am I right or wrong Raghu?"

Raghu nodded unattentionally on it, "No. It's not totally right and everybody loves me it also not true enough. Perhaps, I am bigger than other birds in size and my voice is robust one therefore, everybody fear me, and which you are supposing love and respect that would be not truly love and may be afraidness about me. That reason, perhaps everybody respect me. If you look observely, Kaka neither loves nor repects me. He assumes me a big bird, who want to trying for impression on everybody."

"But, how he had been here?" Lark asked.

"I think, Kaka has said you everything, he had come here because, I had invited him here." Raghu said with smile, "But, I do not know whether you do believe him or not, But, you are a president and you should believe everyone. You could be able yourself for others, only to believe them.Okay. Leave it behind. I was standing outer branch of the tree and looking to great planetory and splendid sky. That time Kaka was flying there and I called him for chating in my tree hole. But, I wondered, why you came to me at the time. It is overturned of midnight and you did not send me any sound -code-message!"

"Have I committed a mistake to come like this?"

"No. Not ever, friend, But, if any bird wanted to meet you at your tree hole, his traveling would be vain and it is night time, it is also not very good for you to travel at the time. If you would have given me any Sound-code-message- I had come to your tree-hole immediately." Raghu talked in explanation tone, "Is any important work?"

Lark remained silent for some time then he hesitatingly went on, "Now, Eaglet ready for hunt. He has been so adept in it that he had never been in past. He has been mature now. And his lots of education has been completed -" Lark stopped for a moment; he was thinking that Raghu would have understood his meaning, but, Raghu only nodded his head.

"Ah .... Now there is a only question which is standing before me, that, what is next? What will be about Eaglet, what is his task now?" Lark asked.

"I have been thinking on this point also. But, I think a question is laid before us and you know well what happens when once offspring bagins to hunt?" Raghu stared at Lark and said .His voice was felt convinced. Lark opened his beak little and asked, "but, would it be proper to do it so immediately?'

"No. it will be not fine yet for that, we have to wait for some time more and in this period we conduct *an examination* for Eaglet?"

"What,? *the examination*?" Lark's voice stuck into in his throat, "But which type of exam?"

"That is very easy, an evalution test for Eaglet about his every subject." Raghu said so easily that it sounded like he was telling any type of joke. "What he have studied yet, those subjectes would be involved in the test and therefore, he must have been adepted and skilled in every subject."

Lark thought for some time, he was looking outward from the doorway in this time, As like he had been gaged.

"What's happened Lark, why you been so silent?"

Lark glanced once on Raghu, "That is an eaglet Raghu. How is his teaching and coaching proceeding, I think, Among of us no one ever have taken this type of training in our life and he is being given Nine or Ten types of coaching at a moment and it is very difficult for him. And over that, It would be injustice for him to face evaluation test (exam) like this." Raghu was looking to Lark who was being emotional and talking ahead, "This age is the golden age of his lfe. At the age he should do linger on pastures or attack on a insects or roll on grass, and we are teaching him how to prepare medicine from shrubs and plants and how to recognise various stars from planetroy. For instance, we are also not able to tell some part of it (we are also unripening in some part of these subjects). At other hand we are weighting on him and after then, his examination......... It is too much for him Raghu........ too much for him........."

"I can understand your trouble Lark; I also have been distracted from this. But, without it we could not find out the progress of Eaglet and it is very important for his upcoming life. You will be pleased that you would take his examination. Believe me!" Raghu said, placing his either wing on Lark's back.

"All is running ahead only on your believe. I have been agreed with your decision. So, when his examination will be begun?" Lark qustioned.

"Very soon, but before that we have to get him some time for practice and preparing. In next week there is The Night of The New Moon, on from that day his examination will be started understood! Do tell this message to our bird -friends and everybody and it is your own duty to tell about it yourself to Mahina and Mooni and tell them there is no causing of worry about it, There all security and protection would be provided to Eaglet and if he succeded in this examination, *then* - "

Raghu stopped for a moment and glimpsed at Lark, who was seemed worried.

"- He will be allowed to stay independently and live freely."

"What?" Lark shouted so laudly that, his voice felt very horrible, *"Koisss Koossisss Kossckssgss."*

Hearing this amusing (unknown) language by Lark, Raghu had to ask for the meaning.

"I said that It would be happened never. He could not stay separate. He will be in great hazard."

"- If this is a matter then, tell me, when you at First hand had been permitted, by your parents to live separate or stay independent, what was your feelings or expression that very moment. were you be happier or sadden? "

For the answer, Lark did not wait for a eye blink-. His face and eyes were telling the truth, "I was so happy, that time that, I had been never ever till now. Onwards from that day, I was going to live with my own accord, and that was a real starting of my life."

"- So, why are you going to pull away this happiest movement from Eaglet, without it how he will stand on his own legs? On from now, he would have to live his life protective and secure, because we can't be with him till last his life. " Raghu made explanation.

"It is different time, although there is still a week for his examination, and untill his examination -" Lark said loudly.

"- Absolutely, he will stay with his parents means Mahina and Mooni, untill he not get success in his examinaton accomplishely, okay?" Raghu accounted.

"But, who will judge the examination? None of exam of this type ever conducted in the Vihangwanah before."

On this Raghu had to get his time for thinkning. Raghu pacing up and down inside the tree hole and thinking deeply. Sometimes Lark opened his beak but soon closed it. He would not want to break the lining thoughts of Raghu.

"I have a thought, we shall elect three judges for the test of Eaglet and they will observe Eaglet's mission (progress) and give him marks. There would be *fourth judge* also, concering about that subject which will be taken an examiation by Eaglet that very moment. Therefore, like this, his progress will be evaluated better way and his examination will be completed very well." Raghu put his view.

Lark nodded his head calmly. The Night was getting darker.......darker........and coolness of wind piercing like ice now.

"- Okay Raghu. I will think about it. It is too late to going on. After some time day will be begun to break. So, now give me bid, I will go to Mahina and Mooni very soon to tell all information about exam and also tell them the fix day of the exam and then with the help of Robin and Gilhary send all the messages about the exam to every bird, isn't it?" Lark said and began to walking towards the wooden swoop but, Raghu called him from back and Lark made turn, "Lark, we will have two judges impartial among them four. Mean neither they both might have taught Eaglet any subject. They two should have tottaly apart from the education and coaching of Eaglet. Therefore, it is your responsibility now, becasue; you are the President of the Vihangwanah. (The Assembly). Good night or I can say Good morning."

"You too." Lark said, he went to the doorway of the tree hole and jumped away outside from there, in lashing cold wind and vague paths, his ahead.

Following day's weather was not just like some previous days. Now, there was a drizzling of rain with bitting cold breezes and the Vihangwanah had come inside the big-black canopy of cloudy sky over. This abruptly rain has messed up a little bit of daily work (routine) of the Vihangwanah. Therefore, Lark had to wait for very long in morning to go to Mahina and Mooni's tree-hole, after respiting on about Six trees, he could managed to reach on the Palsah tree. His body was fully weted with rainy water and he had to keep shaking his wing after some time.

"Examination?" Eaglet shouted more loudly than Lark when, he was standing in fronnt of Raghu, in his tree-hole. Therefore, there was no doubt that, Koel and Sugi who were present on their respective watching duty on the Palsah tree, might have heard it.

"Yes, examination." Lark said silently and shook his body, with showering the water drops on Mahina and Mooni, who were very closed to him, "AOOH....... sorry Mahina.... sorry Mooni, It was unexpected."

"Okay. Okay Lark! But examination!" Mahina said, she casted suggestive eyesight on Mooni, who was shaking his body, because of rain drops but, he also nodded his head, "But, for what?"

"His education has been about to completing now. Therefore, what has he understood and absorbed, it is great time to find out that with the help of light exam. So, his exam is going to begin in the next week on The Day of New Moon and it will proceed Four days after that."

"What? The following New Moon Night?"- Eaglet wondered and asked, "It would be very near."

"You have seven days to practising yourself yet, and I think your over all subjects are Nine (coaching subject), Therefore, you can practice those comfortably." Lark spoke in deciding tone.

"But, Lark, he is too young to do this." Mahina worriedly said.

"In which age we supposed to be young for Eaglet. In that age he would have learnt all and in which age we learn to fly in that age, he could get better hunt. Therefore, if you look at Eaglet now, you can see that, he has been over grown than your size, and reached to mine one. So, it is apt age to observe and learn everything and therefore, we are going to conduct this exam, and he would have to pass it."

"How examination will be executed?" Mooni and Eaglet asked together.

"There will be four judges when you are giving your examination of your respective subjects and your marks depend on how will be your performance."

"- And who will have the judges?" Eaglet asked with cleverly. For a once Lark did look to him and said. "That will be not imparted you, but, which exam you will be giving, that subject's trainer present there as a Fourth judge, I think it will be down your tension, But, other Three judges I have not determined yet."

" - And suppose if I did not succeed in this examination then -" abruptly Eaglet questioned and with this Mahina and Mooni stared to Lark.

"- Then you will have to endure a big trouble in coming days. This is the beginning of the cold air and with following month there will begin *the season of winter,* the coldest one. Therefore, if you have failed in your test then you will have to be given training and coaching of this type for following four months. But, those days could be more bitter than these."

Eaglet shivered with a name of winter and coldness. Because, these days were also with a full coolness. But, now more cold- the chill cold would be fallen very soon in the Vihangwanah and in those days it would be difficult to do hard practice. He knew, it very well it may be a great tragedy if he fall into the river water in fish-catching training in those cold days.

"- And if he passed out the exam-?" Mooni asked.

Lark flummoxed with a question as like he feared that he would be asked this question definitely. But, even, he glanced to Mahina and Mooni and spoke ahead, "Among these all exams one exam will be the exam of hunting. Therefore, once he succeed in it .... and along that, if he succeed in all these exams then ....He will be given a special residence (The tree hole) and then, he will not live with you both further more, he will begin his new life after then."

Eaglet shocked so much, that as like he fell into the *ice-curded-water*. Lark was looking at Mahina and Mooni. But, they both were easy as they were earliar. Having seen it, Lark wondered then Mooni went on, "This is one point, we had expected, when from we had taken the responsibility of him. We knew he would have to live separate from us one day. Therefore, we had been ready for it. But, Lark it will be the only reward he get after his succession in the exam?"

"No not only this one-," Lark said energetically perhaps, he had become very pleased, to see that Mahina and Mooni was not sadened with his information, "-In which subject, he will be merit in the exam, that subject's (coaching and training) will be abolished from his training and coaching. Then he will have only Two subject to learn one is the Woodpeck's alphabet and Sound-code-message and Sugi's, who will teach him how to weave a nest and also Koel is one there but, in not a list yet."

Eaglet pleased to hearing this but, he was disappointed with a idea to live separate from Mahina and Mooni. He never agreed for it therefore, he came some steps ahead and spoke out, "I will never go anywhere from this tree-hole ever."

It was a great blow for Mahina, Mooni and Lark. Lark said, "Listen, once you getting passed from this exam, then you do live alone, means separate somewhere and it is *the imperial law* of the Vihangwanah."

"But, I am not leaving to my parents on any cost, They are my parents. They are, only, who brought up me and gave me the first lesson of my life, everytime they pampered me. so, it is impossible to desert them."

On Eaglet's account Mahina sobed once, Mooni sustained her. Water was shining in her carved eyes. Lark also seemed bewildered. He was finding words to articulate. At the time he stared on eaglet's Amulet and straight on its central-piece, which was colouring Red, "Look, once you did hunt, means -"

"- If my reward for do passing examination will be abondenment of Mahina and Mooni for me, then I prefer to fail in my examinations - then even. If I would have to go for my all trainings in the cold .... blood -frozen cold ....I will not be bothered, but on any condition I never drop out my dear parents ever."

Pin dropped silent spread over inside the tree hole. Mahina was still shedding tears facitly. Mooni patted her with back and simultaneously, kept looking to Lark and Eaglet. But, Lark was not saying a word. At last helplessly, breathing long, he said, "Okay, do we take this decision later, But, please concentrate your task and have your exam with heartly. Therefore, you would have get help in coming days. I leave now, your examination will be begun in next week, mind it and be careful." he took some steps ahead, more close to Mahina and Mooni, "Everything will be all right. He would be totally protected in a course of the exam, bid me now. Robin will come to you for giving the timetable of exam so, Good Bye."

Lark went off from the open wooden- swoop and Eaglet heard his greetings of both the birds, who were on the watching duty by the around trees.

Following *Seven* days were the busiest and the hardest days in Eaglet's life. Sometime rain used to fall and it was the starting of the cold wind also. He was thinking again and again, if all birds decided with mejoritily that he ought to be live with Mahina and Mooni, after been heard his firm decision, then, he will have to practise through these following Four months and he would be transfered into slab of ice very soon , because of chill wind. He was again and again telling himself that, he should not have placed his decision so early, he had to think on that for some more time. But, it was not important one, because, he would have to face upcoming exam with great potential. But, his confidence was not like early days, as it hidden itself somewhere becasue-, he was shot into thorny bush when he was chasing Robin, in his coaching class. Robin had turned around so quickly that without thinking about it, Eaglet Twicely entered into thick bushes, ahead him. It was the worst time for *Star-and-Planetory reading,* and Sona was be more worson than that . These classes were became nightmare for him. Because, it was difficult to follow exact position of stars in cloudy atmosphere and it was more difficult to find out which star was where. Instructing him, more and more, Sona was bewildering him everyday but, it was not only Sona, who was bewildering him with his instructions, but, Safeda, Kite, Dove and other more. They always instructed him and try to lessen his load and tension. But, they were also under heavy tension. Mahina and Mooni were who, had taken the large one. And trying to feed Eaglet lot of without eating (so) much for themselves. They did not instruct him in any case, but only said him that did not take tension and did not worry. Everyone (bird) have to face this type of moment in his life, telling this, Mooni had narrated his own first experience to fly, after that to Eaglet.

Days were flied off ahead. But, those were open days and Rain did not show his favour on the Vihangwanah. Therefore, Eaglet practiced lot of but, did not know why no bird was doing harder work from Eaglet. Although, lovingly behaving with him and Bagga, as like always, behaving with him caringly and affectionetaly. Because now, Eaglet could catch up fish more faster than Bagga could- *("In this my subject, I certain that you will get out of marks." At last, on returning way Bagga told him.)*

Like this subject, he became very adept in the subject of *"Pouncing the hunt"* about it thinking of Sona and Kite was that he definitely going to get great marks in this subject. Safeda, who had been becoming himself prey for Eaglet in practice season, had not said anything. Because, Eaglet pressed his neck with overforced, causing vanished his voice from his throat for sometime.

Preceding day of the examination, Eaglet got his timetable, concerning about exam, by Robin. His exam was to begin on the day of The New Moon and proceeding for upcoming Four days ahead, Robin told everthing oraly and Mahina- Mooni got it into mind as it was. (Because, there were no writing formalities.)

On the first day of his examination was going to start with the exam of Robin's and it was a New Moon Night, he was to give the exam of *study of planetory and stars* at night, on the very first day he was going to unsuccessed, because it was quite hard for him to face the study of stars and planetory. Next day, he had to give three exams of three different subjects. First was the exam of *fish-catching,* second one was the *pouncing on the hunt* and third was *find out the the hazards on land* of Gilhary. There were two exams on day three, that was of *Dove's* and *Safeda's* subject respectively. Those both are quite hard and on the Fourth and last one he was to face the exam of Parinda's subject, which pritise he had been doing from some previous days and it was concern about how to *'find out the correct paths of the unknown parts of the Vihangwanah'.* But, on that very day, the second and last exam, which was, totally strange one and unknown also.

"I don't know anything about last subject's exam how to be performed." when Mooni told him this all, that time he uttered.

"This exam of about find out your presence of mind. Therefore, it will excecuted on the very moment and for that you will have to snitch off any belonging from any flying bird and perhaps, you would have a duel with him. Your marks are on based on, how adepty you do it and also how protectively one." Mooni informed, he was feeling more and more difficult about the exam after, hearing this one. Still his there subjects were poor and now another one subject was going to add it.

"Look here, your subjects will be marked as like" Mahina said and brought him near to Four big different coloured feahters laid on other side and they were heaving with the breeze which came from open wooden swoop. They were different colours: *Red, Yellow, White and Black.*

"Listen, every judge will show you one quill among it after they observed your performance. If you get Red it would be excellant and brilliant, If there will be shown Yellow one, then your performance is best. If you will have white one then supposed that you did satisfactorily and at last If you get Dark-Black, then you would be failed in that subject and that subject supposed to be weak for you and you would have to practice it again. You will have to pass out in mainimum three subjects among these, with best remark. Yellow quills. (Means you have to get six yellow feathers at least.) Then, it will be regarded that you are passed the exam by good marks."

These Four quills were reciting him about his weaked subjects and again and again black feather was sliping off from his eyes. He asked darely, "When I shall be able to look my marks? Instant after my exam?"

"No. No. after the exam, you would have a holiday for one day and then, next day you will come to know what is your marks or result. Then Now I tell you the places, where you are going to give your exams. Preserve it in your mind okay. First place is ....", Mooni was telling him everything, which could be helpful for him at last. He told him that he (Eaglet) would have to go to the spot of exams alone, for every exam.

Thinking over on it, night was come. But, he was not able to sleep. If his father were with him and he living with him then, would he have been given this type of exam too? But, he was not able to find out the appropriate answer either. He had been seeing a big black quill in his dream and again and again he was diving in *cold-chilled-water*.

When he got up very early in the morning, he was feeling like his brain had been numbed. He was total confused and none of thing come in his mind. Mahina and Mooni did not talk very much, as like they were stumped. The time was flying speedly, didn't go like before, with his invisible wings. Whatever Mahina and Mooni gave him to eat, he did not even manage to gulp it as well. After some time he was to depart.But, Mahina and Mooni were not going with him. He himself manage to get Vihangwanah and face the exam of the first subject very soon. The Sun shown his bright face and Eaglet left for his exam, Before it, Mahina blessed him rubbing her beak on his (beak) and Mooni wished him best of luck with blessings. He instantly got out from thetree hole, No one for today, was on watching duty, on neighbouring both trees either. But, he was not felt wondered. He did not have an anxiety for anything now. He just flied away on that direction, where he was to face the first exam of Robin's subject soon.

After how much turning, westing how much time, he reached to that spot, he also unknown himself about that. But, he was there, he suddenly realised about it. There, Robin was waiting for him on the high branch of a *Sandal tree*. He placed himself beside him.

"It is great. You are on time, not earlier not later," Robin floated to him and said happliy, "Judges will arrive soon, are you fearing about exam?"

It was not very easy to nod head in negative direction, but, he nodded it very daringly. There were coming flapping sounds of wings and he witnessed some birds were approaching from air Woodpeck, Parinda, Koel, Sugi, Kaka, Lark, Sona, Kite and also Safeda and Gilhary both standing on grassy land. Instantly, with some fear he came to know he would have been examinated in front of all these birds, not only judges. Which strenght he had recovered till yet, just dropped down now. Everybird friends landed on different tree branches near there. But, Kaka, Lark and Woodpeck reached on top branch of the *Eucalyptus tree* and rested there. They three were judges; Robin put information in Eaglet's ear. So, Kaka was involved into judges, then it had been lessed guaranteed that he could have passed in each subject. If there were Raghu among the judges. it was certain that he would have passed with better ranks. But, It was a clear as The Sunlight that Kaka will give him big black feathers in each and every exam subject.

"Now, I have to go to the judges, I am the fourth judge. Now, listen what work is waiting for you. I have hidden *Ten yellow fruits* in these surrounding various bushes. Attention, every bush is thornful and you collect those fruits on one place, after finding out those. How exactly and how quickly you get collect those fruits, your marks will base on it, other judges have been already informed all this things by me. Do how adeptly you can do it, but protectively. Good Luck."

Robin flied and set himself beside to all three judges, other spectators now were looking at eaglet only. Gilhary and Safeda also conquered on a big bush and gazing at him too. Robin looked to all three judges and waved his head and then he nodded to Eaglet, and he did not have get a second to know that it was a sign of beginning of the exam and then instantly he leaped into air, and heard great sound's of flapping wings around there. Everybird was flapping his wing, while Safeda and Gilhary were jumping on their hind legs, over the bush. He did not much time to look all of them; he was going to every suspecting bushes one by one. He never thought that he could be given this type of task to do, becasue, he till now, always flied behind Robin and this is the way of his practice. But, he never thought how to turn through any thorny bush and search out of hidden something. Now, it was time to prove himself had come and he could have to do that which he had never done in his past days. He kept turning over here and there. He saw a big fruit in the thick bush; he leaped on it and put it down, when he came back from the thorny bush holding it in his beak. He ws turned so, adeptly that he himself felt wondered. He was snooping in every bushes now. He was feeling like that he had been poured some sort of power and now he was feeling everything was easy and handy. He one after another pouncing in five various thorny bushes and collected five yellow fruits on one place, gathered birds were overjoydly shouting for him and flapping enoromously. After then, he found out two fruits from another shrubs. He did not have any idea about his time and no one exactly told him about in how much time he had to collect those fruits. Therefore, he was flying with his blood-and -bone power and he piled out other three fruits from three different elegant bushes.

"Great ! Great ! It's just amazing flying," Woodpeck said, who was a judge, from his place, "No err in anything, just unexpected, Right Kaka?"

Kaka glanced him very spitefully.

Eaglet was again settled on the same branch from where he leapt for his test, some time before. He was panting, little after Dove came close to him and observing, whether he was hurted. When he did over his observation he moved himself to judges and announced, "No injury have been placed on body but, one wing injured little just as like mole, it's ingnorable."

Every bird, who surrounded there, made large flapping sound of their wings, containing Lark, Robin and Woodpeck too. But, Kaka ignored it all and remained indifferent.

"All marks have been delivered to me, they will be shown on the next day after last day of the exam." Lark proclaimed, "Tonight the exam of the *stars and planatory reading* (of Sona's subject) will be held here also, on the nearing, *'Khairaah Tree'*."

"you were just amazing and did that one so speedly that could not have done it so, fast as well." Robin came to him and said enthusiastically, "Now, go to your tree-hole now. Again you have tough exam right ahead you tonight, So Bye, for a moment." He said to Eaglet.

Every bird was beginning to cangratulate him, therefore, he realised that his preformance and flying was outstanding. He was pleased with his heart. When every judge was flying to him, he saw that, Kaka had flied away very long from there and even did not glance behind once.

"Okay now, it is enough, we all shall congratualate him when all exams will be totally concluded. Now, let him go to Mahina and Mooni, therefore, he will able to eat something and rest for some time." Raghu told to everybody in loud voice, when Sugi was trying to meet Eaglet, therefore, Birds left him apart and he could feel free and better. Now, he could see them who were close to him and he was craved for their only sight. Mahina and Mooni were looking at him, from one branch of distant tree and they were looked quite happy. Eaglet spread his overworked wings and reached to them.

"Brilliant, you have carried out great mission, excllent one the God bless you." Mahina went closed to him and behind her Mooni shook his head appreciatelly. Then, giving greetings to everybody, they all Three leaped on air and flying towards their residence. That time Eaglet realised that Raghu was looking towards them but, didn't say anything. Then, he turned away his head other side and with smooth leaped, he was began to flying far and far on the side over skinny branch of *the Bearch tree*. Koel was along with him. But, after that Eaglet could not see them, because, a *big Neem tree* had come in front of his eyes.

He had lot of lunch when he returned in the Palsah tree hole. Mooni also was saying that, he (Eaglet) had overtaken his task so fast that he had not seen anybody as fast as him without Robin. Having heard this his hunger was streched twicely bigger and now he was not worried about anything to come front of him, Although he was going to face off the exam of *the study of reading planetory and stars* the very night. But, Kaka was not seemed very happy on his performance as other birds were become happy. But, he knew that Kaka had been detesting him from very early, by the first appearance of his to the Vihangwanah therefore, he was not going to further worry about Kaka.

His stress, which was on him, suddenly reduced and he was feeling confident, and more better.

The Night was entered in the Vihangwanah, and as though expected, The Moon had been risen in the buest sky, over the forest with resounding of chill and cold windy lashes. He was to go that part alone even this time now, in the dark night. The spot of exam was not far enough, but it was night and he remembered Mooni's words. *"The Vihangwanah becomes more dangerous in the night because, of his changing weather and intricated paths."*

When he flied on the sky from the Palsah tree, he was little afraid about coming exam, but it was totally extuinguished when, he reached to the spot where he respited beside of Sona, Then Sona asked him different types of information about stars and planetory. He was speaking like he was standing in regular classes. He asked him the names of various stars and planets. At this time there were present plenty of birds, but they were standing on distant trees therefore, they were looked vague in darkness. But, which judges were siting on high branch of the tree, they were cleary visible in the white moonlight. Among them, who was the blackish enough he was Kaka; *even moonlight could not lighten him.* Then second was Woodpeck, who is having long carved beak and top crest on his head, and then Lark, they were siting in line. Sona was a fourth judge but, he was asking questions to Eaglet, that reason he had stood with him. He had been still better in his every question. Then he had to go on one tree, which was far away from there, and find out some carvings words and pictures on his trunk (he had been already told by Sona about the words.) and come back after read it. He wasted some time in that but, he successed to come in time. Then, Lark, Kaka, and Woodpeck came near to Eaglet for asked some questions to him on this perticular subject. They asked little one but, most hard too. Therefore, Eaglet had to give stress on his mind for the answers. *(from that he came to known that not only Sona ,who was well informed about the study* of stars *and planetory)* judges were some what satisfied on his answers, but, he knew that his original(real) exam was to come soon, because, Kaka asked his question at last, but even, Sona was not able to give answers of them.

"Which star does help us when we are flying top of the sky, except polar one?"

Kaka understood, by experesions on Eaglet's face, that he could not answer it. but Sona said, "It is not................."

"-Sona, I am the judge here. Therefore, It would be better for you to hear my next question." He moved to Eaglet and asked, "Our shadow does not fall on earth when we flying on, which position The Moon should be that time?" Eaglet nodded directly negative. Threreupon, Sona and other judges were worried.

"You can not ask him these type of questions, it was too deep for me to........"

Did not mind on Woodpeck's speaking a little bit Kaka spoke ahead, "You have asked your questions and I knew very well what was the worth of those questions. I am here present as a judge not a timepasser so, which question I am asking in them some are important questions too. My next question is which three stars come in the line when other stars look -dim?"

Once again Eaglet shook his head disappointedly.

"- It is over then, my question are drained. I will give my marks to Lark." he looked to everybody for once and flied away in darkness.

"He will never be changed, only just one question's answer I can give from his three questions." Sona said when he was looking at that place on which Kaka disappeared before a soft turn.

"Ignore it, your exam was brilliant. It was not troll one." Woodpeck silently said. Once again every birds flapped their wings.

"Tomorrow, you have again exam of three subjects one after another. Today's was great one but, you need rest now, because of your upcoming three exams. Therefore, you come with me; I leave you to your tree hole. Come." Raghu said with coming towards him.

"Okay, for you both good night and you-" Lark moved to Raghu and Eaglet and said, "Best of luck for tomorrow's exams, and today you were really amazing."

Afterthen, having had been greetings to everybody he leaped away with Raghu.. Now he was very easily flying with Raghu. But, he had not in his flying rhythm, like Raghu had and also a robustness of the flying. He had no different colours like Raghu's and even did not have impressiveness of his voice. In all the way, Raghu was complete bird and Eaglet was trying to be like him. He was fond of Raghu when the first time saw him.He realised Raghu was far more than he appeared.

"Why did you be not judge yourself?" Eaglet asked.

"Instead of whom?" Raghu exactly asked.

"Ah................." Eaglet took his time and then imparted, "instead of Kaka".

Raghu laughed on it and they took a turn, "Perhaps, if I were there, I would have given you better marks. You are thinking it, aren't you?"

He only nodded on it, "Kaka is very bad". Put ahead.

"No donbt. But, leave it behind; you need not to think about your marks, other judges give you better one," Raghu mumbled, "Good luck for tomorrow. Look ahead there, I think, I may be looking the Palsah tree and if I do not wrong, I think, Mahina and Mooni standing on the branch and waiting for you outside of the tree hole."

The exam on next day passed away very well, no exam (previous) had been taken place as like this. On early in the morning he had given the exam of *'fish catching'* and the *'pouncing on the hunt',* This time there was not Safeda as a hunt, but Eaglet had to pounced a frog. He extremaly caught the frog as well as he could. Both exams were superbly attened by him. When judges cheared him on his performances, he knew that he was getting full of marks in both exams. But, Kaka was not pleased yet. He did not seem joyable too. The elget was sure that Kaka's marks would not be better than previous one.

Then at the time of evening there was a exam of Gilhary's subject, that was the simplest exam he had ever overcome. In this exam he only had to tell that, from which hazards on the land he would have to protect himself. The judges asked him various types of questions but, Kaka's questions were about Hundred times difficult than any other's. Eaglet had been already guessing that one.therefore, he answered with enough confidence. (But he was not sure that his answers were concerning to the question.) After then, he gave the most difficult exam for him, as he supposed that was Safeda's and Dove's a "*medicinal plants and their uses*" But, it was not as difficult as he was thinking about. He was only asked questions and he also gave it's answer correct one. And also told some names of medicinal plants and their uses. Then which question Dove asked concerning diseases, he also informed very well on that but, he confused many times and did some names of plants here and there. Even then this exam was great, beyond his expectations and Safeda was looking very happy. On the next day which exam was to conduct that's the new subject for him and only two classes was attended by him. This subject was belonged to Parinda and it's about "*the paths of the Vihangwanah*" he had to tell some difficult and strange paths of the forest.For this exam the judges were same but the exam had been held in solitued. Only Parinda, Eaglet and other three judges were present for the exam. In this exam he committed four pinpointed mistakes ("many birds miss their way's when they are travelling through the Vihangwanah, your's were just hair breaking, compare to that." Parinda said to Eaglet when they were travelling towards the "*Palsah tree*"). Eaglet was very happy when he returning, many reason occoured for that, all exams (if do ingore the two exams and marking of Kaka's) were (more) better than he expected. This day was the last day of exam and his last exam was in the evening. This one is totally unknown for him and he knew that he could have to Fight with a flying bird and snitch the thing which he holding in his claws or Biak. He was quite feared that who will be the bird and who might be fighting with him.

When, evening time came and he got out from the tree hole on the Palsah tree, having been the bleessed by Mahina and Mooni. This time he aslo had to go alone in the central part of the Vihangwanah. The night will be fallen soon, he known it and it would be something difficult through nightfall, therefore he leaped and flied with some more power.After having cut off some distance, he had occured to see a bird who was flying some distance ahead and holding Gilhary in his claws. She was seeming as she was in deep sleep. But, that bird was totally unknown and strange for Eaglet, he thought where he was taking away her at the time of evening and quite isolated part of the Vihangwanah no bird was residented here, what was the matter? Eaglet gave himself mommentum and determined to catch the unknown bird; his amulet was swinging with chill wind and striking on his body behind. He reached to them in only ten strocks of his mighty wings.

"Where are you taking up Gilhary and what's happend with her?"

The big bird was not thinking about to be obstacled by any bird, at the moment and it would be quite impossible by any little eagle.

"Mind your onw business." He said, turning beside of a huge *tick tree.*

"Gilhary is the resident of the Vihangwanah and she is unconscious at the moment?" He also turning over the tick tree, "But who are you?"

"I am *a Falcon* and I am taking away her for a treatment, now don't interpute in my work, *saaaricousss kassskass."*

But, by that time, Eaglet already determined something, Although the Falcon was one time bigger than Eaglet. He flapping his wings with speed and went ahead and become a obstacle through the Falcon's way.

The darkness began to fall, wind's speed was slow and his time of the exam had been ending. In which part that exam had been conducted that part of the Vihangwanah was far away from her but, he will not go there leaving all alone Gilhary with the unknown Falcon even though, he had to do coaching in following Four month's, into a cold bone thunder or had to fail in this last subject either. He can't go anywhere from here.

"- So, are you not going from here-" Falcon coldly said, "- do not think like an idiot, you can not Fight with me."

"We shall see it later, but, first you leave Gilhary alone here and after then only you can go from here." Eaglet said courageously, at the moment he first time was to Fight to some stranger bird and it could have been first ever or last one. But, he was great believe on Sona's and Kite's coaching. Suddenly Falcon pounced on him but, by the time he could do himself to move other side and only air of Falcon's wings touched him. He had to take into mind that when, he will attack, he should be not have any injury to Gilhary.

"OH........so you have manouver also, havn't you? Now, show me how you could save yourself from this one." After speaking this, Falcon dropped down Gilhary from his clows. He had been not hoping, some thing like this, would happen... Even then, he swooned down rapidly, there was darkness now and his eyes were only riveted on falling body of Gilhary down, but, on second moment he caught up her with his steely claws. She was still unconscious. But, there was no time to being conscious her, he placed her on one of *Evergreen's shrub* near by, Till now he could not see any flying birds around them and who one was there he had determined to kill him very soon. He heard sound of flapping, Falcon coming down from above. The Moonlight was able to show everything of around them. Eaglet did only know one thing that, whatever happens to him, Falcon ought not to reach to Gilhary. They grappled on one another in air. Their wings rubed on each other, their claws striked against one another and they were begun to attacking on one another.

"From how much hours you learnt how to fly, more than many years I have been hunting." Falcon said with tremendous powered strike on eaglet's wings, that was so speedly attacked that his wing meserably hurt. Now, he could not fly as much as speedly as he was flying earlier. Along that he realised, it was quite hard to Fight with the Falcon.

But he knew that if he had to rescue Gilhary and himself then, it was only way to Fighting better and better, till his win or defeat which, was more certain. He had begun to lashes on the Falcon, but he was very skilled and his striking was more better than little eagle. Both were trying their best, but after some time, Eaglet was tired and his strenght in the wings came to all ends. Now, his one wing and a claw were badly hurted. He also banged on the falcon same destructible stokes but those were not sufficient for his collapse.

The Falcon was conquering more ragingly now and his beak and claws were attacking simultaneously. His first stroke was fallen on his neck (Eaglet's) and murk came in front of his eyes. Then he felt brutal lash on his back, third was on another wings, therefore, now he was not able to control himself. And what was going to happen with him to tell that, there was no need to any prophet. After two or three strokings more. The Falcon was to kill him, Eaglet knew better, and then he would be going away to hold Gilhary with him. He was trying to flapping his wings conrageously. But, it did'not work, he was falling down and down, he will bamp on land very soon and take his last breathe ever. His eyes could be looking on darkness ....gulping darkness......He was definitely was feeling two claws of death on his shoulders (back), It was steely and dark black .... very dark .... like this dark night .... and death.....

****

SEVENTH

Everything was weighted, eyelid were heavy and could not be opened easily. But, he opened it difficultly and saw he was on that place where he had come once in his past. It was a tree hole of Lark, he recognised it, and many bird faces were looking at him and those faces were shining in coming Sunlight, those faces were happy and evergreen like every day. What was happened and how long ago? He did not remember anything. But, Two birds, which were very near to his heart was present by side him, that time he realised he had been (asleep) on rags. Mahina and Mooni were looking at him with as usual caring eyes and Mahina's eyes were watered.

When he was trying to heave, he realised that he was banded some tree leaves on his wings and claws and also something was sticked on his neck, without the amulet one.

"What was happened? How I came here?" he asked. He was not able to recite the past, his head was extremely loaded.

"You are in the Lark's risident tree-hole at the moment and two days have been passed your accident. This is the morning and your health is better now." Raghu, the second bird he liked, came ahead and told, " On that very day, when you did not reach on time for the exam, that time Kite was become worried for you, therefore, he went to Mahina and Mooni for your whereabouts. When he had reached to them he came to know that you had already left for the exam. I accidently happened to know this all and I left for your search. When I reached to you; you had been falling faint and Falcon was about to kill you. But, I saved your life and caught in air and put you down on an Everygreen shrub. Then, I again flied on for the duel with the Falcon, when, Gilhary become conscious, she told me what was happened and how did Falcon swooned on her and trying to hunting prey her. But, you had saved her by the time".

"The Falcon fled away after looked me and Gillhary-," Raghu said easily "- is Okay, but I think, better than okay. She is in his tree hole at the moment and Chidiya is looking after her. She is very very greatful to you. She has been inquiring about your health within each hours and she will be happy after hearing your health is alright now."

Mahina came closer suddenly, her eyes were filled with tears, "You have done a great adventure and proved yourself as original "*Vihangwanahvasi*,"that was really hard and ordeal time for you. But, you amazingly fulfilled it courageously. It was real *examination* for you. It was proudable moment for all of us."

Hearing the word "Examination", the past was come back for Eaglet. He had not attended last (subject's) examination because; he was busy in the dueling with parvenu Falcon, to save Gilhary from his claws. He knew that he could not have absented for any exam on any condition (except death), otherwise, he would have been failed and it was to be happened still now.

"Oh God! I could not give the last exam. Now, will I fail then?" He asked question. He was being afraid, that, his mission to save Gilhary from the Falcon might have been the last exam and it was really true, then, there was no chance for him to pass with a white quill also. But, he was sured now that was not a part of exam. But, was a big danger which fallen on Gilhary, from which he very breavely saved himself and Gilhary too.

"That was impossible, which you have done," Kite said humbly ", - you fought with a Falcon and saved a residence of the Vihangwanah aslo. I could not expect something more than this, If you did not attend the last exam, though you are supposed to be passed the exam. I also did not Fight like you in my whole life ever, you have taken a great decision on right time, even then you knew that there was a little chances for you to exit from the Fight. It was brilliant thinking at your age. Gilhary was an important member of the Vihangwanah. I really thankful to you. I tell you, that Falcons are extremely well Fighters indeed and only the Owls have a might to Fight with them."

"- But, where from a Falcon came into the Vihangwanah?" This efected question by Eaglet, spread silent among birds and they began to look to each other, Woodpeck recovered and told, " Though, any other forest do not exist around the Vihangwanah, but, some times any parvenu try to attack on the this froest. Some birds are thinking to dominate on the Vihangwanah and be the monarch of this prestigious forest. Therefore, this type of attacts used to for us."

Eaglet wondered that he had been lying in this tree hole from Two days. At the moment he realised his result of the examination would have been announced and come to known to everybody. This was now great fear for him, he asked with fear, "Then, my result also would have come to know to everbody?"

"Absolutely, it has been reached to me." Lark said seriously, thereupon, the hotness of The Sunrays in the inside of the tree hole, was felt as increased about ten percent more. Lark went on a other corner, where laid Four feathers of different colours, "I will take names of (subject) and then show you, what marks you have got for your performance. If you have got two black feathers out of four then, you will be supposed to be failed in that subject. You have to pass with three great Red or Yellow feathers, there were four featheres placed here." Lark shown his wings towards heaving feathers, "Red for brilliant and excellant performance, yellow one for best, white for satisfactory performance, and dark-black will stand for fail. So, your first exam was Robin's - "*the speedly movements*", in which your have got three Red feathers and one white from that bird who are not present here at moment. Then next exam was Sona's subject *"the stars and planetory reading,* in which -", Eaglet's heart was beating more fast, "Execpt Kaka one other judges gave you three Red feathers and Kaka shown (gave) you black one." On this gathered bird were flapped their wings and sweared some words about Kaka's bad marking, but Lark waved them for silent and spoke ahead-.

"- Then you given the exam of *"Fish catching*" of Sona, you have got three Red quills in that and Kaka gave you white one, next was Gilhary's subject to "*Find out the Hazards on land*," you have got better marks, other three judges shown you Red feathers, but, Kaka - shown you the black feather -" On this, Kaka's decision also badly sweared by gathered birds and they canvassed lot of because, this exam was the easiest exam for Eaglet, "- Then next both exams were about "*medicinal plants and their uses*" of Safeda and also Dove's subject, in this exam, marks were given by combinely by all eight (four and four) judges.. Two judges - I will not take name of any judge - give him yellow feathers and other four shown him Red feathers. In these both exams - *Kaka*- because he did not forbid me to take his name before you, gave one white and one black quill for each exam. Then, there was a exam of Parinda's subject in that, Eaglet has scored Three Red feathers from three judges and black one by Kaka. ("- *Like his heart and colour."* Bagga whispered to Sona, some surrouding birds laughed on it.)

"Then the last, but not in the least exam- which was not exactly or truely exam but, the ordeal for Eaglet, in that Woodpeck, Kite, and Lark - means I - have given him Red feathers (Because, you did not have much better marks than this." Sona said loudly and everybird shook his head, Lark too) *but Kaka* - "Once again Lark stopped his speaking, "- gave the black quill because, You (Eaglet) did not reach for the exam, on the spot there."

Now, on this point, every bird complaining about Kaka's marks in loud voice. They had not discussed so loudly before some time.

"Though Kaka have given eaglet very bad marks in other exam , yet he (Kaka) ought to have given Red or yellow feather for the last one." Koel said in his sweet voice, though his voice was flooding with full of spite, "This is not a matter only about Eaglet's exam but, about his courage and sacrifice for a member of the Vihangwanah. If any other bird were present instead of Kaka there, he would have definitely shown Red feather for his courage. Kaka has not done right."

On this description every gathered bird waggled their heads, Eaglet saw around him, but he could not see the black face of Kaka among other birds. Execpt Gilhary and Chidiya, every member of Vihangwanah was present there, Safeda stood on his hind legs, and, Eaglet knew it that must be Safeda who operated him by his accident. (Battle with Falcon.)

"But, I am thinking why he was made a judge?" Robin asked with rage.

"Because, he was the ex-president of the Vihangwanah and he also was a nutral judge, we did not have any option without him. Therefore, he was selected as a judge." Lark defined.

"Without, it, he is a brilliant bird too." Raghu said

He spoke something at first time. At this time he was appearing bigger and more colourful. Perhaps, the Sun was starting to rising up at the moment and the light inside the tree hole was increasing.

"How many incidences could you remember of that day?" Bagga questioned him.

"Nothing, Falcon stroked on my neck about two times and those were so strong that darkness had come in front of my eyes, then, black something........."

"Would not a black, but would be something five coloured." Sona said, "- Becasue, then Raghu saved you."

"May be.......but ...."

"- I think that was a night time and you were badly hurted. Your eyes also closed that reason, when your eyes opened for only moment you could see my silhouette there, in black colour." Raghu said.

He shook his head, Raghu was right. Because, he was so, badly hurted that he could not do open his eyes. This happening once again made remember him about that rainy night when he reached to the Vihangwanah and he had seen somebody standing by side him in night, but did not remember who was that. His father or any other bird of the Vihangwanah either.

It was deep evening now and the tree hole of Lark about emptied and without him, Mahina and Mooni was present there. Mahina even did not budge from him, for whole day, she was still gazing at Eaglet, like only his gazing was able to recover him from bad injuries. Lark and Mooni were standing in another corner of the tree hole and was busy in conversation, looking that, Eaglet asked Mahina, "Far how many days we shall stay here?"

"For more some days untill your wings and claws do not recover well." She said, "Lark permitted us that we can stay here as long as we want?"

"- And what's about our old tree hole?"

"Nothing. Lark goes for sleep there for night, and in the day time it is closed."

"- and Gilhary?"

"She was feeling better now. Her swelling on legs going to down and she will be able to walk very soon. Safeda infromed us." Mahina, satisfactorily said, "He had come from her."

"My other exams, did you see those?"

"Absolutely, we have witnessed your many exams, but I alway afraid that if you got hurt by any performance But, you were excellent and which rank you have got in exam that is unbelievable also." Mahina talked smoothly, "Raghu gave us information that he had never seen anybody to get so great marks which you have absorbed in your exams. And what did you last one........ All Vihangwanah knew it very well!"

Month September was begun and four days were passed away very soon. Woodpeck came and gave a *birch-tree-leaf* to Mahina and Mooni, on which he had written (inscribed) Eaglet's marks, was accordingly his subjects. (Marks had been written with colours as Red, Yellow, White and Black and with name of exams and judges respectively.) Untill, Gilhary recovered totally and she had visited Eaglet twice with a help of Safeda. (Kite helped her to climb in Lark's tree-hole) The marksheet was currently kept in Lark's tree hole and many birds suggested to cut off the marks which were given by Kaka (or on Ninth subject either.)

There was not made any another attack after the first one. The Falcon was not found by anybody, when they were searching every corner of the Vihangwanah. Kaka had not shown his black face in the Lark's tree-hole or in Gilhary's either, Eaglet was not despleased with it. He also did not want to see that black face again. Then, On one evening, Lark told him that in following days there was to be held a big banquet in the Vihangwanah and Eaglet's name was to be cristianined as "*Vainteya*"(called Eagle in Sanskrit) because, he passed out in every examination with great marks and also did the great job without the exam one. When, he would totally recover, after then, the banquet was to be held following month. He was to learn two subjects among these nine, according to Kaka's markings and some more training session he would have to attain of another (different) subjects.

Having heard this all news he was overjoyed with happiness. He did not know the reason. But, he was be mature now and grown up. He was to be given the same prestige and dignity which his father had. Every bird and animal now agreed his superiority. He was glad. Very soon he was to be called out as eagle, though from following month his training and coaching was going to begin again or that was a starting of *The Winter season* with ending of this one, meant the Rainy season. The next season was very hard and bad for him as well as for Vihangwanah. But, it was a circle and law of the nature that Rainy season ends and winter begins. The season of mist and some more challenges. But, Eaglet known very well that hard time goes and comes simple or easy one and again easy time goes and comes harder ....

He was about to go ahead, it was his luck that what was going to happen in next month. But, yet he excited but amazed hearing that in this night time, the tone of a "*Miya malha*r *Raga*" was being piped from somewhere in the *Reed forest* nearby meant, he had some more days in his hand yet to enjoy the rivalry of *The Rainy season*..........

www.ingramcontent.com/pod-product-compliance
Lightning Source LLC
LaVergne TN
LVHW041215150826
845673LV00001B/416

* 9 7 8 9 3 8 4 3 1 4 0 1 9 *